William Samuel Harris

The Harris Family

Thomas Harris in Ipswich, Massachusetts,1636

William Samuel Harris

The Harris Family
Thomas Harris in Ipswich, Massachusetts, 1636

ISBN/EAN: 9783744754378

Printed in Europe, USA, Canada, Australia, Japan

Cover: Foto ©Raphael Reischuk / pixelio.de

More available books at **www.hansebooks.com**

THOMAS HARRIS,

IN IPSWICH, MASS. IN 1636. AND SOME OF HIS

DESCENDANTS,

THROUGH SEVEN GENERATIONS,

TO 1883.

BY

WILLIAM SAMUEL HARRIS.

PRINTED FOR THE AUTHOR, BY
BARKER & BEAN, NASHUA, N. H.
1883.

CONTENTS.

Introduction.   .   Page 1

PART I.

Chapter I. Origin and Meaning of the Name.—The Family in Great Britain.—Early Emigrations to America.   .   .   Page 5

Chapter II. First Generation in America.—Thomas Harris.   .   .   .   .   .   Page 9

Chapter III. Second Generation.—Serjeant John Harris.   Page 18

PART II.

Richard Harris, Third Generation, born Ipswich, Mass., 1705, died Harvard, Mass., 1776. And a Full Account of His Descendants, Male and Female, through Five Generations, to 1883.

Chapter IV. Third Generation.—Richard Harris. Page 25

Chapter V. Fourth Generation.—Martha Harris (Wetherbee).—Her Descendants.   .   .   Page 29

Chapter VI. Fourth Generation.—Jacob Harris.—His Descendants.   .   Page 31

Chapter VII. Fourth Generation.—Richard Harris, Junior.—His Descendants.   Page 56

Chapter VIII. Fourth Generation.—Rebecca Harris (Scollay).—Her Descendants.   Page 73

Chapter IX.   Fourth Generation.—Nathaniel Harris.—
    His Descendants.   .   .   Page 88
Chapter X.   Fourth   Generation.—William   Harris.—
    His Descendants.   .   .   .   Page 104

Additions.   .   Page 127

Index I.   To Names of Harrises in Part I. (Chapters
    I. II. III).   .   Page 129
Index II.   To Names of Descendants of Richard Har-
    ris². (in Part II),   .   .   .   Page 130

PORTRAITS.

1. WILLIAM-SAMUEL HARRIS[7] [No. 136.] . . Frontispiece
2. RUTH (PRATT) HARRIS [No. 33.],
    SALLY (HARRIS[6]) COULT [No. 59.],
    EDWARD-PRATT HARRIS[6] [No. 60.],
    SAMUEL HARRIS[6] [No. 63.],
    JOHN-MILTON HARRIS[6] [No. 71.],
    JACOB HARRIS[6] [No. 74.], *and*
    WILLIAM-CALVIN HARRIS[6] [No. 80.],   Faces Page 37
3. GEORGE-CALVIN UNDERHILL[7] [No. 133.], ... 53
4. SAMUEL SCOLLAY[5], M. D. [No. 235.], ... 75
5. JASHER HARRIS[3] [No. 459.], ... 106
6. GEORGE-WASHINGTON HARRIS[9] [No. 517.]   112
7. WILLIAM-MARTIN LOREE, SR. [No. 534.],
    and HARRIET-MARY (RHODES[6]) LOREE
    [No. 534.], ... 116
8. WILLIAM-HARRIS RHODES[6] [No. 549.], ... 119

OTHER ILLUSTRATIONS.

1.   Seal of Dea. John Staniford,   Page 14

2.   Autograph of Serjt. John Harris²,   ··   20

3.   Sketch of Dea. Jacob Harris⁴,   ··   30

4.   Autograph of Dea. Jacob Harris⁴,   ··   30

5.   Silhouette of Samuel Scollay⁵, M. D.,   ··   74

6.   Autograph of Samuel Scollay⁵, M. D.,   ··   75

7.   Loom-Harness Factory of George-W. Harris⁶,
     Lowell, Mass.,   ·· 112

8.   Autograph of George-W. Harris⁶,   ·: 112

CORRECTION.

On pages 20 to 64, wherever the name *John*¹ occurs, (as the father of Serjt. John²,) it should always be read *Thomas*¹.

INTRODUCTION.

"Honor thy Father and thy Mother."

This Record and History of one small branch of the Harris Family in the United States is now completed, and is sent forth to the members of the family—now scattered all over the country—with the hope that they will with interest peruse its pages, which will afford them much information not otherwise obtainable.

The main portion of the book, or Part II., consists of an account of the descendants of Richard Harris[3] of the third generation in America, son of Serjt. John[2], and grandson of Thomas[1] and Martha (Lake) Harris of Ipswich, Mass. All the descendants of Richard[3] are traced down to 1883 through all the lines of descent, male and female,—with the exception of the descendants of his oldest child Martha[4] (Wetherbee). Concerning this branch I have been unable to obtain much information, and do not know whether any representatives of it are now living or not.

In the winter of 1874-5 I commenced to collect information regarding the Harris family—or rather to record facts given by Miss Eunice Harris[5] and others. In the beginning of 1877 I commenced tracing the descendants of Richard[3] in the different branches, and have since continued this work as time and opportunities have been found, until the work is now completed and the records are printed.

The vast amount of labor required in preparing a work of this kind, even one of limited extent, is hardly imagined by those who have had no experience. The writing of hundreds of letters to persons all over the country, the examining of family, church, town, and county records, and the copying and arranging in proper order the facts thus collected, require a large amount of time, labor, and patience. This has been a work for which I can never receive adequate pecuniary returns. Yet it has been a pleasant work ; and the thought that in thus gathering from the shadowy past and the perishing present the records of lives spent in honor and usefulness and transmitting these records in imperishable form to the future, something was being done for the good of the family and mankind,—this thought has been an incentive to patient labors.

We have a noble and honored ancestry : and in this fact we not only may but should rejoice with that true pride which shall incite to worthy deeds, that the virtues of the fathers may be perpetuated in the children. The later generations of the family—those now living—are worthy of their honored ancestors, being men and women of true characters, intelligent, respected, and useful. So far as my knowledge extends, the family are inclined to the nervous temperament. Perhaps this History is deficient in not describing as fully as would be desirable, the traits of character, virtues, and qualities of mind and heart possessed by the various members of the family. But this would be hardly proper as regards the *living* members : and my object has been rather to give a family *record*,—an exact record of births, marriages, and deaths, and of all *events* of interest and importance.

This History will be found to be, in an unusual degree, complete, full, and accurate in details, particularly in dates of births, marriages, and deaths. With very few exceptions the *exact* date is given in all such cases. The *full names* are also given in the case of *every* member of the family.

Mistakes are inevitable in works of this kind, but if any errors are found in this book, the fault must rest with those who furnished me the records, as I have used *extreme* care in copying and arranging the dates and facts furnished, and in printing them. Readers will confer a favor by sending me the correction of every error which they discover in the book.

It will be seen that no Harris descendant in the fifth generation—grandchild of Richard Harris'—is now living, the last surviving representative having been Eunice Harris' see Nos. 24, 52.], who died in Windham, N. H., June 18, 1877. The widow of Dr. Samuel Scollay[8] [see Nos. 230, 235,] is however still living in Smithfield, W. Va., and alone represents the generation. The *ninth* generation from Thomas Harris consists of three members, Nos. 227½, 618, and 620.

ARRANGEMENT.

The plan on which this book is arranged is simple, and will be easily understood after reading the following explanation. Following the name of each Harris descendant (in the coarse type) is a small figure which shows the *generation* to which the person belongs, counting from Thomas Harris', the emigrant ancestor from England. Thus Richard Harris was of the *third* generation, or the grandson of Thomas'.

In Part II., commencing with Richard Harris' as No. 1, consecutive numbers are used at the left margin of the page running through the book, by means of which all persons are easily referred to, no two persons having the same number. Each Harris descendant comes in first as a child in fine type under the account of his or her parents: here the name, dates—and often places—of birth and death are given, but usually nothing further. If the child became the head of a family, or if there is a special account of his or her life, it is given farther on in the book in coarse type. In such cases the person has *two* numbers; and following each person's name in each place is his or her *other* number in brackets [ ]. For example, on page 45, No. 89 is Mary-Cordelia Sprague'—daughter of Cordelia-Esther Moore' (Sprague)—whose date and place of birth are there given, and the number [137, is the number she bears as the head of a family. Turning to No. 137 on page 54 we find Mary-Cordelia Sprague', and the number [89,] refers back to her place as a child.

Following each person's name in the coarse print is a list, enclosed in parenthesis ( ), of his or her ancestors back to Thomas Harris'. Thus in the example referred to on page 54, Mary-Cordelia Sprague' was the daughter of Cordelia-Esther Moore', whose *married* name was Sprague; *she* was the daughter of Martha Harris', whose married name was Moore; Martha', was the daughter of Dea. Jacob Harris', who was the son of Richard', son of Serjt. John', son of Thomas' (wrongly given as John').

The first and second names of persons are connected by a hyphen, thus distinguishing middle names from surnames. Where persons appear at the head of a paragraph in coarse type (as in the example referred to) the *surname* is always given if it is different from Harris; where no surname is

given, Harris is always to be understood in the coarse type.
In the fine print no surname is ever given, but is to be found
in every case from that of the father in the account just
above.

ACKNOWLEDGMENTS.

My thanks are extended to all who have assisted in this
work by furnishing whatever information it was in their
power to give. For thus helping to preserve the history and
records of the family in its different branches they deserve the
thanks, not only of myself, but of every one who has any
interest in the family; and they have aided in a work which
will endure and increase in value as the years go by. The
various persons to whom application was made for information generally responded readily and with interest.

I ought especially to mention as helpers the Misses A.-B.
and M.-B. Harris[5] of Warner, N. H., who furnished a large
amount of information concerning Dea. Richard Harris[1], Jr.
and his descendants; and Mrs. Elizabeth Page[6] of Clarksburg, W. Va., who collected most of the facts concerning
Dr. Samuel Scollay[7] and his descendants. Augustine Caldwell of Worcester, Mass., George-B. Blodgette of Rowley,
Mass., and others, have given me much valuable assistance.
Those who so generously contributed to furnish portraits of
themselves or others for the embellishment of the book deserve
the thanks of all. I may here say that the origin of this
History depended largely on information given by Miss
Eunice Harris[5] of Windham, N. H.

WILLIAM-SAMUEL HARRIS.

WINDHAM, NEW HAMPSHIRE, SEPTEMBER 1, 1883.

THE HARRIS FAMILY.

PART I.

CHAPTER I.

ORIGIN AND MEANING OF THE NAME.—THE FAMILY IN GREAT
BRITAIN.—EARLY EMIGRATIONS TO AMERICA.

ORIGIN AND MEANING OF THE NAME.

The name Harris is of *Welsh* origin, and means "The son
of Harry." From "English Surnames, an Essay on Family
Nomenclature" by Mark-Antony Lower (London, 1875) we
learn :—

"Those who are conversant with documents belonging to
the middle ages, are well aware of the disposition that then
existed to make the father's Christian name the surname of
the child." "In England, when the *patronymic* was used,
the word *son* was usually affixed, as John Adam*son* : in Wales,
on the contrary, although the staple of the national nomenclature was of this kind, no affix was used, but the paternal name
was put in the genitive, as Griffith William's, David John's or
Jones, Rees Harry's or Harris."† After mentioning a list of
"English surnames which have been derived from baptismal

*Vol. I. p. 160.   †p. 19.

names," among which is "Henry," the author says:—"Great
numbers of these have been assumed in the genitive case, as
John Reynolds, for John the son of Reynold, James Phillips,
for James the son of Philip."'

The addition of the letter "s" or the syllable "son" to a
Christian name, or the prefixing of "Fitz" (a corruption of
"fils") or of "Mac", has the meaning and effect of "the son
of." Harris, then, as a surname is of Welsh origin, and
means "The son of Harry."

Harry is a diminutive or nickname of Henry. Webster
gives as diminutives of Henry, "Hal, Harry, Hen, (Hawkin,
obsolete)." In the list of surnames derived from baptismal
names in the work above referred to is the following para-
graph† :—"From Henry are derived Henrison, Harry, Harris,
Herries, Harrison, Hal, Halket, Hawes, Halse, Hawkins,
Hawkinson, Halkins, Allkins, Haskins, Alcock (?), Hall
(sometimes)."

Henry as a Christian name is given by Webster as of Old
High German origin, and as meaning, "The head or chief of
a house." Ainsworth gives the meaning as "Rich lord."

THE FAMILY IN GREAT BRITAIN.

The name Harris is found in "A List of sixty of the most
common Surnames in England and Wales in 1838" in the
work on "English Surnames" above referred to. In the number of births of persons bearing the name, during the year
ending June 30, 1838, the name of Harris stands the twenty-
fifth, in deaths, the twenty-fifth, and in marriages, the twenty-
seventh.‡

In a letter dated June, 1881, the Postmaster of Chelmsford,
England, says:—

"There are branches of the family in every county and
town; it is an old name and a very prolific one; and in Wales

the name appears to be more plentiful than in any other part of the United Kingdom."

A letter from the Postmaster of Merthyr Tydvil in Wales, dated August, 1881, states that the Harris family in the Principality is "legion: it is one of the most common names next to Jones and Williams." The family there (in Wales) are of the middle class, chiefly trades-people and the like.

EARLY EMIGRATIONS TO AMERICA.

The families of Harris in the United States are very numerous, and can not be traced to a common ancestor, as many *distinct* emigrations of persons bearing the name appear to have taken place at a very early period in the history of New England. Previous to 1640, many of the name were in New England and were among the early settlers of different towns.

The remainder of this chapter is largely extracted from Savage's Genealogical Dictionary of New England Settlers.*

Walter Harris came in 1632 from Norwich, England, in the "William and Francis" to Weymouth, Mass.; in 1649 he was of Dorchester, Mass., and in 1652 removed to New London, Conn., with his wife and sons.

William Harris was in Salem, Mass., in 1635, and removed with Roger Williams to build Providence, R. I., in 1636. His brother Thomas settled in Providence in 1637.

George Harris was in Salem, Mass., in 1636; and Arthur Harris in Duxbury, Mass., in 1640.

THOMAS HARRIS and his wife Elizabeth were among the early emigrants from England to Massachusetts. They were in Charlestown, Mass., in 1630.† After the death of Thomas his widow married, 2, Dea. William Stilson, of Charlestown,

---

*The reader is referred to that work for fuller information concerning the Harrises mentioned in this chapter, and others of the name.
†Wyman's Genealogical History of Charlestown.

and died Feb. 16, 1670. In 1680 Dea. Stilson testified that
Thomas Harris kept the ferry from Boston to Winnisimet
(now Chelsea) and Charlestown, 49 years before, and that he
(Dea. S.) married the widow of Thomas Harris and continued the ferry. This is the oldest ferry in the United States.
Thomas and Elizabeth Harris had sons Anthony and William, and Anthony in his will, in 1651, mentions brothers Daniel and Thomas, and brother-in-law Elias Maverick, who married his sister Ann.

John, Thomas, and William Harris were among the first
settlers of Rowley, Essex Co., Mass., in 1644, and Daniel
came soon after; each had a two-acre house-lot laid out to
him. The lots being of two acres each, shows that they were
all men of property and importance. These four house-lots
were all adjoining each other, which would indicate that they
may have been brothers; and Daniel and William were cer-
tainly brothers.

It is *very probable* that all the following early settlers of
New England were Thomas and Elizabeth Harris's

CHILDREN, BORN IN ENGLAND.

1. Anthony, of Boston, Mass., was son of Thomas and Elizabeth; belonged
    to the artillery company, 1644; was in Ipswich, 1648; died in Chel-
    sea, Mass., 1651; mentions no children in his will.

2. Daniel, of Rowley, Mass., about 1645, is supposed to have been the
    brother of Anthony. About 1652 he removed to Middletown,
    Conn., and died 1701. He had ten children, the oldest born in
    1651.

3. John, of Rowley, Mass., in 1644, may have come from London in 1635,
    aged 28. He is supposed to have been brother of Anthony. He
    had six children (see page 18, foot-note); died in Rowley, 1695.

4. Thomas, of Ipswich, Mass., in 1636, is supposed to have been the brother
    of Anthony. He married, 1647, Martha Lake; died 1687. He was
    the ancestor of the Harrises mentioned in this book. See Chap-
    ter II.

5. William, of Charlestown, Mass., in 1642, was the brother of Anthony and
    Daniel, and was probably brought in youth to Massachusetts by his
    parents. He had five daughters, the second born in 1646. He af-
    terwards removed to Middletown, Conn., and died in 1717.

6. Ann, the sister of Anthony, married Elias Maverick before 1651.

CHAPTER II.

FIRST GENERATION IN AMERICA. — THOMAS HARRIS.

THOMAS HARRIS[1], was *probably* the son of Thomas and Elizabeth Harris [see Chapter I.]; yet as he himself was undoubtedly born in England and emigrated to this country, he is considered in this book as Thomas[1] of the *first* generation in America, the first emigrant ancestor of the Harrises whose history is here given.

He was one of the early settlers of Ipswich, Essex County, Massachusetts, being in that town as early as 1636, three years after its first settlement. If he was of age in 1636 he was born *not later* than 1615, in England.

In 1644 he seems to have been living in Rowley, an adjoining town, of which he was one of the first settlers. In the first laying out of lands in Rowley, "the tenth of the eleaventh Anno Dni 1643", that is, Jan. 10, 1644,† he had land

---

*By mistake, *John*[1] is given on pages 20 to 64 as the first ancestor, the father of Serjt. John[2]; in all these places it should read *Thomas*[1].

†Previous to 1752 the years commenced on March 25; consequently a record of Feb., 1740 (for example,) — or Feb., 1740-1, as it was sometimes written, means Feb., 1741, according to the present mode of reckoning. By act of Parliament in 1751 England adopted the Gregorian calendar, and the year 1752 was made to commence on Jan. 1. To correct the inaccuracy of the former mode of reckoning, Sept. 3, 1752 was called Sept. 14. These changes—to which the terms "old style" and "new style" refer—must be borne in mind in examining ancient records. In this book the *years* are given corrected to agree with present usage. The days of the month, however, in dates copied from ancient records, are given as there found, and without the addition of eleven days which is necessary to make them conform to the present or new style of reckoning.

laid out to him as follows:"—"To Thomas Harris one house Lott Containinge two Acres, bounded on the South side by John Harris his house lott, the East end by the streete": a planting lot in the "Northeast Field" described as "eight Acres of vpland, lying vpon the North side of William Harris, butting vpon the abovesaid places": "one Acre and a quarter" in "Satchells Meadow": "two Acres of Salt Marsh" at "Warehouse River": two acres at "Sawyer Island": one acre at "Cowbridge": two acres at "Newbury Highway": and two acres near "Long Island."

He sold all his estate in Rowley in 1644, and settled in Ipswich, where he remained during the rest of his life. In 1651 Thomas Harris of Ipswich, "seaman", and Martha his wife gave a deed confirming the sale of 1644.

He was one of the twenty Ipswich men who went in 1643 as soldiers against the Indians, and who, for their service, were each "allowed 12 d. a day (allowing for the Lord's day in respect of the extremity of the weather)". He was tithing-man in 1677: died in Ipswich, August 2, 1687.

Thomas Harris' married, Nov. 15, 1647, Martha Lake, daughter of John and Margaret (Read) Lake. She belonged to an aristocratic family, and Thomas Harris' must have been a man of quality and good standing, or he could not have married her. His *two*-acre house-lot at Rowley also shows him to have been a man of property and importance.

"John Lake descended from the Lakes of Normanton, Yorkshire, who claimed descent through the Cailleys from the Albinis, Earls of Arundel and Sussex, from the Counts of Louvaine (the right line of Charlemagne), and from William the Conqueror".[+]   Mrs. Margaret Lake, mother of Martha (Harris), was the daughter of Edmund Read of

---

* "Book of Grants" of the town of Rowley, Mass.
[+]Heraldic Journal, vol. 4, p. 74.

Wickford, Essex County, England. Her ancestry can be traced back to 1534.* She came to New England, and was the first white woman who went to New London, Conn. She was there (with her brother-in-law John Winthrop, Jr.,) the first summer the settlement (called Pequot) was commenced, 1645. She seems to have lived much with her sister Mrs. Winthrop, but her later years were spent in Ipswich. John and Margaret (Read) Lake had three children:—1, John, who probably remained in England; 2, Anna or Hannah, who married Capt. John Gallup, celebrated for courage in fighting the Indians in the Pequot war and who was killed in the Narragansett Swamp fight, Dec. 19, 1675; 3, Martha, the youngest, who married Thomas Harris[1].

Mrs. Margaret Lake died in Ipswich, in 1672, between Aug. 30, and Sept. 24. The following is a copy of her will entire, dated Aug. 30, 1672, and proved March 31, 1674:—

"In the name of God Amen.

"I, Margaret Lake of Ipswich in America, in the Shire of Essex Widdow, being weake in body, yet of good and p'fect memory and vnderstanding praised be God doe dispose of that little estate God hath lent mee as followeth.

"Inprimis. I give and bequeath vnto my Daughter Hannah Gallop and her Children all my Land at New London. And also my best gowne and my red cloth pettycoate, and

*William Read of Wickford d. 1534; his son Roger of W., d. 1558, was father of William, b. 1540, in W., d. 1603; his son Edmund of W., b. 1563, d. 1623, by wife Elizabeth had seven children, born from 1595 to 1614; of whom Margaret, b. probably about 1600, m. John Lake and d. 1672, in Ipswich, Mass. Margaret's sister Martha m., 1. Daniel Epps; m., 2. Dep. Gov. Samuel Symonds; d. 1662, in Ipswich, Mass. Their youngest sister Elizabeth, bapt. in W., Nov. 17, 1614, d. 1672; m. John Winthrop, Jr., the founder of Ipswich, Mass., and first Governor of Conn. Their brothers remained in England; two named Edmund d. young, William and Thomas m.

Many more facts of interest concerning Mrs. Margaret (Read) Lake and her relatives can be learned from Savage's Dictionary; Ancestry of Priscilla Baker, by W. S. Appleton; Heraldic Journal; Mass. Hist. Soc. vol. 1, series 5; and History of New London, Conn., by Miss Caulkins.

my enamiled ringe, and after her decease my will is that my grand Daughter Hannah Gallop shall haue the said ringe.

"Also I giue vnto my Grandaughter Hannah Gallop a paire of Sheetes, and one of my best pewter platters, and one of the next.

"Item I give vnto my Daughter Martha Harris my Tapestry Couerlet, and all my other apparell which are not disposed of to others pticulerly.   Also I give vnto her my mantle, and after her decease to all of her children as they may neede it. Also the Couerlet of Tapestry after my Daughter Marthas decease, I giue it to my Grand Sone Thomas Harris and he dying without Issue, to his Brother John, and so to the rest of the children.

"Also I giue to my Daughter Martha my Gold ringe, and my Will is, that after her decease, that my Grandaughter Martha Harris shall haue it.

"Item I give to my Grandaughter Martha Harris my bed and bedsted and one boulster, tooe blanckets tooe pillows, and one Couerlett.

"Item I give to my Grandaughter Elisabeth Harris one heyfer at my Cosen Eppes.

"Item I give to my Grand Daughter Margaret Harris my Couerd Box and one Damaske Table Cloth and six Damaske Napkins.

"Item My Will is that all my Brase and pewter, with the rest of my household stuffe vndisposed, be equally disposed and diuided amongst my Daughter Harrises Children.

"Item I giue and bequeath vnto my Sonne Thomas Harris, all the rest of my Estate, viz: my part of the vessell, and all my debts, &c (onely my Byble excepted, which I give to my Grand Sonne John Harris', and a paire of frenged Gloues. And Appoynt my Sonne Thomas Harris and my Daughter

---

His grandson John Harris was Serjt. John[2], and by his will in 1728 he gave his "Great bible"   probably this same one—to his son John[1] [see page 20.]. Does any one know its later history?

Martha Harris to bee my Executor and Executrix of this my last Will and Testement, this thirtith day of August, in the yeere of Grace sixteene hundred Seuenty and tooe. 1672.

"MARGARET LAKE

"hir marke."

"these being Witnesses

"THOMAS KNOULTON sen^r

"JAMES CHUTE."

There is on record "A trew Innetory of the Estate of Mrs. Margrit Lake Ipshwich in the Countie of Esex written in the yere of our Lord 1672 Desember the 24." from which "the totall sum" of her property appears to have been 147 £ minus 3£ 9s. 7d. of debts to be paid. The land which she gave to her daughter Gallup "before she made hir will" was not included in the inventory. The following are a few of its items :—

```
"Itum one Tapshire Courclit    -    -    4 - 10 - 9
A Scarlit mantill    -    -    -    -    4 - 00 - 0
A Damask tabel cloth and six Napkins 4 - 00 - 0
A great Bibell    -    -    -    -    -    0 - 12 - 0
Two Gould Ringes -    -    -    -    3 - 10 - 0
8th parte of the Barke    -    -    -    12 - 00 - 0"
```

Thomas' and Martha (Lake) Harris had the following

CHILDREN, BORN IN IPSWICH, MASS.

1. Thomas, b. Aug. 8, 1648, d. "beyond sea" before 1687, as appears from the will of his father, who had given him forty pounds to redeem him out of Turkey.

2. Martha, b. Jan. 8, 1651, d. probably between 1672 and 1696.

3. John, b. Jan. 7, 1653, d. Nov. 21, 1732. See Chapter III.

4. Elizabeth, b. Feb. 8, 1655, married John Gallup before 1696.

5. Margaret, b. Aug. 6, 1657, d. May 18, 1750. She married, before 1680,
    Deacon John Staniford* of Ipswich, who died May
    27, 1730, aged 82. They had nine children, born
    from 1680 to 1698. (See Ipswich, Mass. *Antiqua-
    rian Papers*, May, 1882.) A picture of Dea. John
    Staniford's seal, 1694, is heregiven.

6. Mary, b. Jan. 31, 1660, d. probably before 1696.

7. William,‡ b. Dec. 12, 1661, d. Dec. 31, 1751.

8. Ebenezer, b. probably in 1663, married, Sept. 15, 1690, Rebecca Clarke,
    and had children.

Thomas Harris' died in Ipswich Aug. 2, 1687. The following is a copy of his will‡ entire, dated July 16, 1687, and
proved Sept. 24, 1689 :—

"In the Name of God Amen. The 16th day of July & in
the yeare of Grace *1687*. I Thomas Haris of Ipswich in the
Shire of Essex in New-england doe make & declare this
my last will & testament in writing revokinge therby both
in deed & in Law all other former wills & Testaments. I being
at this time weake in body, but of good & pfect memory
(blessed be God) first I comend my soule into the hands of
God my maker hoping assuredly through the onely meritts of
Jesus Christ my Savio' to be made ptaker of life everlasting, &
I comend my body to the earth wherof it is made to be de-
cently buried by my loveing wife Martha Harris whome I
make & ordaine my sole executrix of this my will & testament,
my Just debts to be paid by her out of my estate : And the
remainder I give as followeth.   Inprimis I give & bequeath
unto Martha Harris my Deere & loveing wife, my dwelling

*Madame Rebekah Symonds, widow of Dep. Gov. Samuel Symonds of
Ipswich died 1695; her will, dated July 15, 1695, contains the following items :—
"I Giue unto my Cousine Martha Harris, a good new Scarfe of Equall vallue
with my best scarfe." "I Giue unto my Cousine John Staniford one of my
Gould rings and Three pounds in mony."   She calls them cousins "proba-
bly because a former wife of Mr. Symonds [Martha Read.] was their aunt."

‡Perhaps this William died in infancy and the William who grew up was
born Dec. 12, 1664, as both dates of birth are on record.

‡The original will can be seen in the Probate office, Salem, Mass.; also
the original petition of Mrs. Martha Harris.

house & Barne & the orchyard, & gardin, & three marsh
Lotts at Plumb Island. And also I give unto her two third
p^{ts} of my Planting lott on middle Island, & also the hither
part of my planting lott at Towne on the south side of the
highway as far as the old fence, & all that planting lott on
the North side off the highway afore named, & also I give to
her one halfe of the Claypitt meadow, And two thirds of my
marsh lott at the hundreds with my part in the boate, Also I
give unto her fower Cowes, & fower Oxen, with all my Sheepe
& Swine; and all my househould stuff with the Instruments
& utensills of husbandry whatsoever duringe her naturall life.
More over my will is that my Loveing wife may give & dispose of all my household stuffe & other things not mentioned
in this my will at her pleasure amongst o^r Children. Item
I give unto my sonne John Harris & to his heirs forever, The
new house which I built in Ipswich, also I give to him & his
heirs forever my two marsh lotts purchased off Deacon Good-
hew at Plumb Island, and that part of my planting lott at
Towne from the old fence to Samuell Graves his pasture after
my debts be paid, Also I give unto my sone John & to his
heirs for ever one third part of the planting land at Middle
Island, and two oxen, And halfe the Clay pitt meadow, And
one third p^t of my marsh in the hundreds for quantity &
quallity, And more over I give to my sonne John & his heirs
forever, after his mothers deseace one third part of the house-
lott & orchyard, & my will is that my sonne John shall have
one third p^t of the fruit of the orchyard during his mothers
life yearly.

"Item after their mothers deseace I give to my sonne William Harris & Ebeneser my younger sonns, the three marsh
lotts at Plumb Island, & halfe the Clay pitt meadow, & all the
planting land which their mother enjoyed during her life:
And also two third parts of the house lott & orchyard, And
two third parts of the marsh lott at the hundreds for quantity
& quality. Also I give my two sones William & Ebenezer

my dwelling-house & Barne with the Comonage belonging to
the same, with the shop betweene them, to them & their heirs
forever after their mothers deseace. my will is that if any of
the brothers be minded to sell their part of Land or Meadow
that the other brethren may have it giveing as much as an
other will give.   As for my oldest sonn who dyed beyond sea,
I gave him forty pounds to redeeme him out of Turkie which
I account was his portion.   In witness wherof I have heere
unto sett my name & seale.

"THOMAS HARIS."   [SEAL.]

"Witnesses,

    "DANIEL EPPS sen^r

    "JAMES CHUTE sen^r"

Jan. 1, 1696, Mrs. Martha Harris petitioned the Judge of
Probate as follows :—

"Martha Harris Widow Relict of Thomas Harris Late of
Ip^r dec^d & Exex of his Last will & Testament

        "Humbly Sheweth

               "That my s^d Husb^d. did in his
s^d. Last will & Testament devise & bequeth vnto his sons
Jno. William & Ebenezer all his Reall Estate & vnto my self
all the psonal Estate during my natural life Inabling me to
giue & dispose of ye same at my pleasure among our Children.—Now for as much as there are two other Children of
my s^d. Husb^d. & mine (to witt) Elizabeth the wife of John
Gallop & Margaret the wife of John Staniford wch. are not mentioned in my s^d. Husb^{ds}. will wch so fell out by the fault of
him that wrott the same—I do therefore Humbly Request
yor Hon^{bl} approbation that I may settle upon our two sd Daughters Equally the moueable Estate aboue mentioned Except
what I shall necessarily Expend for my Comfortable main-
tainance & suport during my naturall Life as apprehending
the same to be Just & Equitable they being my Husb^{ds}. and

my Children as well as any of the others which I hereby
aver & offer to be deposed on my oath of the same

"Martha H Harris."
her
mark

Mrs. Martha (Lake) Harris probably died before April 5,
1700.

CHAPTER III.

SECOND GENERATION.—SERJEANT JOHN HARRIS.

SERJEANT JOHN HARRIS[2]* (Thomas[1] [see Chapter II.]), the third child of Thomas[1] and Martha (Lake) Harris of Ipswich, was the father of Richard[3], whose descendants are traced in Part II. of this book. He was born in Ipswich, Mass., Jan. 7, 1653, and seems to have spent his life in that town. He married, in Ipswich, Jan. 8, 1686, Grace Searle, daughter of William and Grace Searle† of Ips-

---

*There were *four* John Harrises in Ipswich at the same time as early as 1696, each with a family, namely :—Marshal John[2], with wife Esther in 1673; Serjt. John[2], who married Grace Searle in 1686; John with wife Mary in 1690; and John Harris, Quartus, with wife Margaret in 1696.

Of these, Marshal John[2], or Under Sheriff, a locksmith or gunsmith, who married Esther ———— — and died in Ipswich Sept. 15, 1714, was the son of John[1] and Bridget Harris of Rowley [see Chapter I.]. This is proved by a deed (recorded Essex Deeds 1 Norfolk, 277.) in which John[1] of Rowley in 1663 bought certain lands in Haverhill, and another deed (Essex Deeds 5 Ips., 117.) in which John[2] with wife Esther sold the same lands in 1685; and the will of John[1] in 1692 says that he had already given these lands to his son John[2].

This Marshal John[2] was born Oct. 8, 1649, and by wife Esther or Hester had eight children, born in Ipswich from 1673 to 1691,—the oldest was John[3].

Serjt. John[2], who married Grace Searle and died in 1732, was the son of Thomas[1], as is proved by a deed (Essex Deeds 15 : 49,) in which "John Harris, husbandman, William Harris, smith, and Ebenezer Harris, husbandman," all of Ipswich, sold in 1695 a portion apparently of the land given them by the will of Thomas[1] their father, and in the acknowledgment, made April 5, 1700, the words occur, "Then Sarjt. John Harris" etc.

†William Searle had three children :—

1. Samuel, elder son.

2. William, younger son; born in Ipswich, Nov. 22, 1665; died in Rowley, Nov. 7, 1690; His estate amounted to $8. 18s. clear. "In Court at Ipswich held by adjournment Nov. 3, 1691, ye Inventory was psented by ye administrator, John Harris."

3. Grace, married Serjt. John Harris[2].

William Searle, Senior, died in Ipswich, Aug. 16, 1667. His widow Grace married, 2, in Ipswich, Oct. 26, 1668, Thomas Dennis. Augustine Caldwell of Worcester, Mass., has a pillow-case spun, woven and made by her, with

wich.   He seems to have lived ever after this in Ipswich, and died there November 21, 1732, "Otatis 82."[†]   "Grace Harris, relict of Serjt. John Harris," died June 10, 1742, in Ipswich.[†]   Ipswich is an important town in Essex County, Massachusetts, midway between Salem and Newburyport; it was first settled in 1633.   The village is about a mile from the sea on Ipswich river, which is ascended to this point by small vessels.   Rowley joins this town on the north.   Serjt. John[2] and Grace had the following

CHILDREN, BORN IN IPSWICH, MASS.

1.   John, b. Dec. 18, 1686.[‡]   See below.
2.   William, b. Nov. 26, 1690.[†]
3.   Rebecca, b. Jan. 11, 1693.[†]   See below.
4.   Samuel, b. April 9, 1695.[†]
5.   Martha, b. Dec. 2, 1698.[†]   See below.
6.   Daniel, b. Nov. 22, 1700.[†]
7.   Richard, baptized Nov. 25, 1705.[†]   See Chapter IV.

Serjt. John Harris[2] was called a fisherman in 1699; was first called Serjt. that year; was a commoner in 1707.   August 23, 1728, Serjt. "John Harris of Ipswich, yeoman, being grown aged, but of perfect mind and memory," made his will[‖] of which the following is a portion:—

"Item.   I give and bequeath unto Grace my Well beloved Wife the whole of my household Goods of what sort soever, absolutely and to be Intirely at her dispose.   Allso I give unto my Wife the use and Improvement of my whole Estate, during the time She shall remain my Widow.   Leaving the whole in her hands for her more Comfortable Subsisttance dureing the time of her widowhood.   Item.   I give unto my Daughter Martha the Privilege of Possessing and Improving

her initials beautifully embroidered upon it.   The grave-stones of Thomas and Grace Dennis are to be seen in the High St. cemetery, Ipswich.   Their daughter Elizabeth Dennis married a Hovey, and was an ancestor of Augustine Caldwell, to whom the reader is referred for further information concerning the Searles and other Ipswich families.

[†]Ipswich Town Records.
[‡]Records in office of Clerk of the Courts, Salem, Mass.
[‖]The original will can be seen at the office of the Register of Probate, Salem, Mass.

for her own use the parlour Chamber in my now Dwelling
House : and a Conveniance in my Cellar for so long time as she
shall remain unmarried. Item, my Will is that at my Wife's Decease the whole of my Estate whether Reale, Personal or
moveable Common Right &c. that is not before Disposed of in
this my Will shall be honestly & Justly Apprised and Equaly
divided among my Children, to each an Equal Share Except-
ing son John unto whom I give five pounds more then unto
Either of his Brethren, and allso my Great bible." . . . .
"And I do hereby Constitute make and ordain my now Wife
my Sole Executrix of this my Last Will and Testament and
at her decease my Will is that my Son John Harris shall suc-
seed as an only and Sole Executor of this my last Will and
Testament." It was further provided that the son John[2] should
pay the funeral expenses of Grace, out of the estate before division.

Serjt. John Harris[2] "dyed Nov. 21, 1732, Otatis 82." The
will was "proved, approved and allowed," Dec. 18, 1732, being presented by the Executrix. The widow Grace Harris
died June 10, 1742. A fac-simile of the autograph of Serjt.
John Harris[2] is herewith given, a copy of the signature to his
will, written Aug. 23, 1728.

THIRD GENERATION.*

1. John[3] (Serjt. John[2], John[1]), is undoubtedly the one who
married Elizabeth Cows of Ipswich : their intention of marriage was published Oct. 26, 1717.

CHILDREN, BORN IN IPSWICH, MASS.

1. John, baptized Sept. 28, 1718.

. . .

*No attempt has been made to trace the decendants of the children of Serjt.
John Harris[2], except those of his youngest child Richard* [see Chapter IV.].
But what facts concerning the others have been noticed are here given.
Those interested are referred to the Town Records of Ipswich, from which
more can probably be learned.

2. Agnes, baptized Oct. 4, 1719.
3. Giles, baptized. Oct. 6, 1723.*

3. REBECCA[3] (Serjt. John[2], John[1]), was probably the one who married William Wilcomb of Ipswich,—their intention published Sept. 11, 1725,—and died in Ipswich, Feb. 10, 1726.

5. MARTHA[3] (Serjt. John[2], John[1]), perhaps never married. Her father speaks of her as unmarried in his will, in 1728. She perhaps removed to Harvard, Mass., in 1743 with her brother Richard[3] [see Chapter IV.] as "Martha Harris, aged person," died in Harvard, March 9, 1782.†

7. RICHARD[3] (Serjt. John,[2] John[1]). See Part II. of this book for a full account of him and his descendants to 1883.

---

*"Gyles son of John Harris Serjts.' son and Elizabeth." "Agnis, daughter of John and Eliza. Harris, jur."—Ipswich Town Records.
†Harvard First Church Records.

PART II.

RICHARD HARRIS, THIRD GENERATION,

BORN IPSWICH, MASS., 1705   DIED HARVARD, MASS., 1776

AND

A FULL ACCOUNT OF HIS DESCENDANTS, MALE AND FEMALE

THROUGH FIVE GENERATIONS,

TO 1883.

CHAPTER IV.

THIRD GENERATION.—RICHARD HARRIS.

1. RICHARD HARRIS[3] (Serjt. John[2] [see Chap. III.], John[1] [see Chap. II.]), was the seventh and youngest child of Serjt. John[2] and Grace (Searle) Harris of Ipswich, Mass. He was born in Ipswich ; baptized there November 25, 1705. He died in Harvard, Mass., December 20, 1776, aged 71 years and 26 days.† From this it would appear that he was born Nov. 24, or subtracting eleven days, Nov. 13, old style, 1705.

He lived in Ipswich until 1743, when, his parents being dead, he removed with his family to Harvard, Worcester County, Mass., a beautiful and excellent farming town on the east bank of the Nashua river. Feb. 4, 1743, Richard Harris "Weaver" deeded to Thomas Hovey 3d of Ipswich, Fisherman, "a Certain Tract or Parcel of Tillage Land, containing Three full acres, situate, lying and being in the North Division of Turkey Hill Eight and ye Eight next Rowley," "for and in consideration of ye sum of One hundred and Five pounds in Bills of Credit of ye old Tenor." This deed was signed by

RICHARD HARRIS.

her
MARTHA X HARRIS.‡

mark

"May 26, 1743, Jer. Foster and Rich'd Harris of Ipswich bought of Benj. Morse of Harvard, 112 acres of land situated

*Ipswich Town Records.
†Harvard First Church Records.
‡Essex Co. Records, Salem, Mass.

in Stow on the west side of the river bounding on Lancaster and Lunenburg lines."[*] This Jer. Foster was perhaps a connection of Richard Harris' wife.

The reason of Richard Harris' removal from Ipswich to Harvard is as follows, according to tradition :—Ipswich being near the sea, in fact a sea-port for small vessels, many of its inhabitants were fishermen and sailors, and many of the young men naturally developed tendencies for a sea-faring life. To prevent his sons from becoming sailors, by removing them from the locality where an inclination for such a life was very likely to be developed, to an inland town at some distance from the sea, he removed to Harvard in 1743 when his oldest living son Jacob[4] was two years of age. The homestead where he resided in Harvard is thought to have been without doubt the one later occupied by his son Richard[4], Jr., situated midway between Harvard Center and Still River village. [See No. 141.]

A list of the members of the First Church of Christ (Orthodox Congregational) in Ipswich, made April 21, 1746, shows that the church then numbered 304 members, among whom were ·Richard Harris and his wife."[†] Richard Harris[3] was dismissed in 1758 ·from his partic. Relation to ye Chh." in Ipswich, ·in order to his being admitted into ye Chh. in Harvard,"[†] and he united with the latter Nov. 13, 1758.

Richard Harris[3] married, 1, probably in the summer of 1735, Martha Foster. ·Richard Harris and Martha Foster, both of Ipswich, were published the 10th day of May, 1735."[‡] Martha, daughter of Jacob and Martha Foster, was born in Ipswich, December 16, 1710.[§] She died in Harvard, September 8, 1756, aged 46 : ·a good woman."[¶] Richard[3] and Martha Harris had the following ten

---

*New England Historical and Genealogical Register.
†Ipswich First Church Records.
‡Ipswich Town Records.
§·Dec. 16, 1710."—Ipswich Town Records.
¶Harvard First Church Records.

CHILDREN.

2. Martha   [12].   baptized in Ipswich, Mass., April 11, 1736. Married John
                      Wetherbee.   See Chapter V.
3. Richard   baptized in Ipswich, Mass., March 5, 1738.   Died in Ips-
                      wich, April 16, 1738.
4. John   baptized in Ipswich, Mass., August 12, 1739.   Died in
                      Ipswich, February 20, 1740.
5. Jacob   [17].   baptized in Ipswich, Mass., February 15, 1741.   Died in
                      Windham, N. H., September 26, 1826.   See Chapter VI.
6. Richard [111].   baptized in Ipswich, Mass., April 3, 1743.   Died in Har-
                      vard, Mass., June 27, 1798.   See Chapter VII.
7. John   baptized in Harvard, Mass., October 20, 1745.   Died in
                      Harvard, September 21, 1756.
8. Rebecca [229].   born in Harvard, Mass., March 25, 1748.   Baptized in
                      Harvard, March 27, 1748. Married Grover Scollay. Died
                      in Rindge, N. H., March 21, 1819.   See Chapter VIII.
9. Anna   baptized in Harvard, Mass., April 29, 1750. Died in Har-
                      vard, November 28, 1750.
10. Nathaniel [333]. born in Harvard, Mass., April 4, 1752.   Baptized in Har-
                      vard, April 5, 1752.   Died in Brandon, Vt., June 21, 1831.
                      See Chapter IX.
11. William [414].   born in Harvard, Mass., October 8, 1754.   Baptized in
                      Harvard, October 13, 1754.   Died in Grafton, Vt., Au-
                      gust 30, 1831.   See Chapter X.

Martha, first wife of Richard Harris[3], died, as above stated,
September 8, 1756.   Richard Harris[3] married, 2, Mrs. Phebe
Atherton, the widow of John Atherton of Harvard.   Phebe
Wright of Andover, Mass., married, 1, July 1, 1730, John
Atherton.   They settled "near Harvard Meeting-house."   He
died previous to December 17, 1755, as at that date his widow
and Richard Harris[3] rendered their account of the administra-
tion of her former husband's estate.   "John Atherton and his
wife Phebe Atherton (now Harris)" joined the Congregational
church in Harvard January 13, 1734.   She died in Harvard,
July 21, 1795, aged 82.   Richard[3] and Phebe Harris had no
children.   John and Phebe Atherton had ten children.[*]   One

*John and Phebe (Wright) Atherton had the following children:—
  1. John, b. about 1735, who m. Hannah Cole: 2. Samuel: 3. Ezra: 4. Elia-
kim: 5. William: 6. Thomas: 7. Phebe, who m. in Harvard, Feb. 19, 1752,
Henry Willard, Jr.: 8. Lois, who m. in Harvard, Feb. 19, 1752, Grover
Scollay [see No. 229] and died in Harvard Sept. 7, 1778: 9. Sarah: 10. Lydia
bapt. Oct. 30, 1747, who m. Richard Harris[3], Jr. [see No. 6, 111.]

daughter, Lois, married Grover Scollay, who married, 2, Rebecca Harris[1]. [See No. 8, 229.] Another daughter, Lydia, married Richard Harris[1], Junior, brother of Rebecca[4].
[See No. 6, 141.]

CHAPTER V.

FOURTH GENERATION. — MARTHA HARRIS (WETHERBEE). —
HER DESCENDANTS.

12. MARTHA HARRIS' [2.] (Richard', Serjt. John',
John'), was the oldest child of Richard' and Martha (Foster)
Harris: she was born in Ipswich. Mass.: baptized there
April 11, 1736. In 1743, her father with his family removed
to Harvard, Mass. She joined the Church (First Congregational) in that town, May 25, 1755. She married, in Harvard, March 25, 1760, JOHN WETHERBEE. One child of John
and Martha' Wetherbee, named Martha', was baptized in
Harvard, March 1, 1761. Her neice, Miss Eunice Harris
said that John and Martha' Wetherbee lived in New York
State, and had children, Richard', Jacob' and Eunice'.
Nothing further than this has been learned of them or of their
descendants, although diligent inquiry has been made among
families named Wetherbee and Wetherby in New York and
other states.

CHILDREN.

13. Martha, baptized in Harvard, Mass., March 1, 1761.
14. Richard.
15. Jacob.
16. Eunice.

Jacob Harris
1789

The original of the above likeness of Dea. Jacob Harris'
[Nos. 5, 17,] was drawn in 1826 in Windham, N. H., after
his removal to that town, and consequently but a short time
before his death. Dea. Harris was then 85 years of age. As
he was sitting in church one Sunday, Silas Dinsmoor of
Western New York who was visiting in Windham, observed
the aged gentleman and sketched what was pronounced an excellent likeness on the cover of a psalm book,—which is now
in the possession of Miss Harriet Dinsmoor of Windham.

The autograph given above is a fac-simile of one written
in 1789 in a psalm book which is now owned by the author
of this book, William-S. Harris' of Windham, N. H.

CHAPTER VI.

FOURTH GENERATION.—JACOB HARRIS.—HIS DESCENDANTS.

17.   Jacob Harris [5.] (Richard, Serjt. John, John)
was born in Ipswich, Mass.; baptized there Feb. 15, 1741:
his father removed with his family to Harvard, Mass., in
1743 when Jacob was two years old.   Jacob when a young
man left Harvard and settled in Ashburnham, Mass., where
he married and lived the most of his life.   He was a farmer;
lived a mile and a half north of Ashburnham Center village,
a little more than a mile from Meeting-House hill,† and in
full view from the cemetery on the top.   The place is now
owned by Mrs. Townsend Barrett and occupied by Joshua-T.
Stowell.   The house which Jacob Harris' undoubtedly built
is now standing, a large, low, one-story house, facing south
in a beautiful situation with Meeting-House hill in sight
towards the south, and the noble form of Monadnock moun-
tain towards the northwest.   Here he lived with his son Jacob
Jr. until the spring of 1826, when they sold the farm and removed to Windham, New Hampshire.   He was the ancestor
of all the Harris family connected with the town of Wind-

---

*His daughter Eunice said he was *born* Feb. 15, old style, or Feb. 26, new
style, 1741.   The Ipswich Town Records record his *baptism* as Feb. 15, 1740,
which means 1741.

†On the top of this high hill is a level space; here is the cemetery of the
town, and here stood the old meeting-house, whose ridge-pole formed a water-
shed between the Merrimack and Connecticut rivers.   On this elevated hill-
top, beautiful in summer with its extended prospect, the people of the town
assembled for worship until 1834, when a new church was built in the village
below.   There was no stove in the old meeting-house until the winter of
1825–6.   Near the middle of the cemetery are the graves of Rev. Jonathan
Winchester and his wife, the three wives of Dea. Jacob Harris', and two of his
children.

ham. He died in that town, Sept. 26, 1826, aged 85½ years, and is buried there. He joined the Congregational church in Ashburnham in 1769; in 1788 he was chosen Deacon which office he held until death. In 1778 he held a town office, "Committee of Correspondence," which doubtless related to the war.

Jacob Harris' married, 1, Oct. 26, 1769, Elizabeth Winchester, daughter of Rev. Jonathan and Sarah (Craft) Winchester.* She was born in Brookline, Mass. June 20, 1751, and died June 21, 1782, aged 31. She joined the church in Ashburnham in 1769.

CHILDREN, BORN IN ASHBURNHAM, MASS.

18. Betsy   [25]. b. Sept.25, 1772; d. May 30, 1865.
19. Samuel [33]. b. Aug. 18, 1774; d. Sept. 5, 1848.
20. Jacob   . b. April 3, 1777; d. Oct. 5, 1778, in Ashburnham.
21. Sally   . b. June 20, 1779; d. Oct. 11, 1820, in Ashburnham.

He married, 2, August 21, 1783, Mrs. Anna-Merriam Warren, widow of Samuel (?) Warren. She was the daughter of Samuel and Anna (Whitney) Merriam,† born in Lexington, Mass., Oct. 10, 1753, died Sept. 13, 1790. She married, 1, Samuel (?) Warren and had two children, Annie

*Rev. Jonathan Winchester was the first minister of Ashburnham, installed pastor the same year the church was formed, 1760. He was highly esteemed; died in office greatly lamented, Nov. 26, 1767, aged 50. His widow Sarah died in Ashburnham, July 27, 1794, aged 69.

Miss Charlotte-E. Harris' of Windham, N. H., has a wine-glass which belonged to Rev. Mr. Winchester, her great-great-grandfather. William-S. Harris' of Windham has a piece of the wedding-dress in which Sarah Craft was married to Jonathan Winchester, May 5, 1748; in the same dress their daughter, Elizabeth Winchester was married to Jacob Harris', 1769, and their daughter Betsy Harris' was married to Jonathan Merriam, 1798. [see Nos. 18, 25.]. The dress thus served as a wedding dress for *three generations*. It was of figured white silk, very rich and handsome. He has also a plate which is supposed to have been owned by Mrs. Winchester, and successively by her daughter Elizabeth Harris, her daughter Betsy Merriam', and her daughter Betsey-M. Harris⁶. He also has among his collections of family relics and antiquities a pair of silver sleeve-buttons which were owned and worn by Jacob Harris', his great-grandfather.

†The Merriams of this country descended from Joseph¹, son of William Merriam of Hadlowe, Kent Co., England. Joseph¹ and his brothers Robert¹ and George¹ came to America about 1635 or 1636; settled in Concord, Mass. His son Joseph² settled in Lexington. His son Thomas' died 1738 aged 66. His son Thomas⁴ was baptized April 21, 1700. His son Samuel⁵, b. Lexing-

and Rebecca who married Levi Whitney. Anna Merriam was a sister to Jonathan Merriam who married Betsy Harris[5] [see Nos. 18, 25.].

CHILDREN, BORN IN ASHBURNHAM, MASS.

22. Martha [46], b. June 10, 1784; d. Nov. 11, 1865.
23. Jacob   [51], b. Nov. 14, 1786; d. Feb. 27, 1860.
24. Eunice [52], b. Jan. 28, 1790; d. June 18, 1877.

He married, 3, Oct. 11, 1792, Mrs. Ruth Pratt of New Ipswich, N. H., widow of Edward Pratt.* Ruth Pool* was born in Fitchburg, Mass., Aug. 24, 1751, died Nov. 11, 1817, aged 66. She married, 1, her cousin Edward Pratt; he settled in New Ipswich with his father—whose name was Edward†—and died March 27, 1781. They had three children‡, Edward, Ruth, who married Samuel Harris[5] [see Nos. 19, 33.], and John. The three wives of Jacob Harris[1] died in Ashburnham and are buried on Meeting-House hill.

ton, Dec. 21, 1723; m., June 4, 1752, Anna Whitney; lived in Lexington and Westminster, Mass. Their children were:—

1. Anna, b. Oct. 10, 1753; m., 1, Samuel (?) Warren, m. 2, Jacob Harris[1]. [See Nos. 5, 17.]
2. Eunice, b. June 22, 1755; m. John Fessenden.
3. Samuel, b. March 25, 1757; m. Elizabeth Fessenden.
4. Ruth, bapt. Feb. 25, 1759; m. Richard Graves.
5. Tabitha, bapt. Dec. 28, 1760; m. Thomas Johnson.
6. Nathan, bapt. April 29, 1764; m. Abigail Holden.
7. Jonathan, b. Feb. 16, 1766; m. Betsy Harris[5] [see Nos. 18, 25.].

For further information concerning the Merriam family in the United States those interested are referred to Dea. A.-H. Merriam of Templeton, Mass.

*The Pratt and the Pool (or Poole) families are said to have descended from ancestors who came from England and settled in Reading, Mass.

W.-S. Harris[5] of Windham, N. H., has a small sampler worked by "Ruth Pool, May the 1, 1768."

†Edward Pratt, senior, died about 1800. He had three sons:—

1. Nathaniel, settled in Reading, Vt.
2. Edward, m. Ruth Pool as above stated; settled with his father in New Ipswich, N. H.; d. March 27, 1781.
3. John, settled with his father in New Ipswich after his brother died.

‡The three children of Edward, Jr., and Ruth (Pool) Pratt were:—

1. Edward, b. 1777, a physician; settled in Maine; d. there March 10, 1811, unmarried.
2. Ruth, b. Aug. 29, 1779; d. March 22, 1869; m. Samuel Harris[5] [see Nos. 19, 33.].
3. John, b. Aug. 30, 1781; d. April 9, 1848, in Windham, N. H.; has numerous descendants in Mass. and N. H.

FIFTH GENERATION.

25.   BETSY[2] [18.] (Dea. Jacob[4], Richard[3], Serjt. John[2],
John[1]). married. Feb. 13, 1798, JONATHAN MERRIAM of Gardner. Mass. He was a brother to Anna-Merriam Warren.
who married Jacob Harris[4] [see Nos. 5. 17.]. He was the
son of Samuel and Anna (Whitney) Merriam. born in Lexington. Mass., Feb. 16, 1766 : died in Gardner. Jan. 13, 1825.
They lived in Gardner. Mass. until Mr. Merriam died. He
was a farmer and shoemaker. After his death his widow
lived a year at her father's in Ashburnham. then went to
Fitchburg in the spring of 1826 : lived the rest of her life
there. and died there. May 30, 1865, in her ninety-third year.

CHILDREN, BORN IN GARDNER. MASS.

26.   Jacob-Harris, [53]. b. Jan. 22, 1799.
27.   Nathan. b. Aug. 7, 1800, d. Sept. 19, 1805, in Gardner.
28.   Betsey-Winchester, b. Aug. 7, 1802, d. Sept. 16, 1805, in Gardner.
29.   Sally-Harris, b. Oct. 18, 1804, d. Aug. 17, 1838, in Fitchburg.
30.   Samuel-Harris, b. May 16, 1808, d. Dec. 2, 1824, in Gardner.
31.   Milton, b. June 20, 1810, d. Jan. 19, 1825, in Gardner.
32.   Betsey. [58], b. Nov. 17, 1813.

33.   SAMUEL[5] [19.] (Dea. Jacob[4], Richard[3], Serjt. John[2],
John[1]). was born in Ashburnham. Mass., Aug. 18, 1774 :
died in Windham, N. H., Sept. 5, 1848, aged 74. He lived
in Ashburnham until his marriage in the spring of 1798. then
moved immediately on to a farm in the western part of Fitchburg. Mass. He joined the First Congregational church in
that town Nov. 17, 1799, his wife uniting May 3, 1801. Feel-
ing called to devote his life to the Christian ministry he moved
his family back to his father's in Ashburnham in the spring of
1801, and went to study for the ministry with Rev. Samuel
Worcester*, his pastor in Fitchburg : he studied divinity with
Rev. Seth Payson† of Rindge, N. H. He commenced
preaching as a candidate at New Boston. N. H., and received

*D. D. in 1811 ;—a brother to Jesse Worcester. the father of Joseph-E.
Worcester, LL. D., the lexicographer.
†D. D. in 1809 ;—father of Rev. Edward Payson, D. D.

a call to settle as pastor of the Presbyterian society. This
he at first accepted but on account of opposition of the Ar-
minians he withdrew his acceptance. He seems to have
preached alternately at New Boston and Windham, N. H.,
about a year, commencing in June, 1804. In June, 1805 a
call was extended to him to settle as pastor of the Presbyterian church and society in Windham. He accepted, and was
ordained and installed Oct. 9, 1805, by the Presbytery of
Londonderry. At the ordination the Introductory Prayer was
made by Rev. Samuel Worcester of Salem, Mass., the one
with whom Mr. Harris had studied in Fitchburg; and the
Sermon was delivered from I. Cor. 2 :2 by Rev. Seth Payson
of Rindge. He received an annual "salary of $400, and a
small settlement."

"Mr. Harris continued the pastor of the church and society
respected and beloved of his people, a little more than twenty-one years, and was dismissed Dec. 6, 1826, in conse-
quence of losing the use of his voice, and having been for a
long time [a year or more] unable to preach. During his
ministry the number added to the church was about sixty-
eight." Eleven ruling elders were ordained. The town in
Nov., 1826 voted to dismiss him "on account of his inability
to perform ministerial duties, the organs of speech having
failed him." "His ministry was successful in building up the
church and in bringing it to a higher standard of piety and
Christian discipline. It was blessed with a powerful revival
of religion in 1822, which was the first general revival oc-
curring in town. Of this work it is remarked that the whole
community seemed moved; every family was stirred, and it
seemed as if the people would go to meeting continually;
and the objector expressed his fears that the crops would not
be attended to. A large number were gathered into the
church, which from that time became decidedly Evangelical,

*Windham Session Records.

and reformed from its former Arminian tendencies."[*]

The meeting-house in which the Rev. Mr. Harris preached is now the town house : it was erected in 1798. In the spring of 1806, a few months after Mr. Harris was settled in Windham, a movement was started to establish a circulating library, the first in town, and he was the first of the three trustees, chosen Aug. 28, 1806. He was a member of the Committee for Inspecting the Schools (consisting of one in each of the six districts) for seven years between 1809 and 1827. He was a member of the Superintending School Committee (which consisted of three persons) in 1846 and 1847.[†]

After his dismission at Windham he recovered the use of his voice and was able to supply in other places, but was never settled again. He preached for the Trinitarian Congregational church in Dublin, N. H., two years, and for the (then) Presbyterian church in Hudson, N. H. two years : he also preached a short time in Sharon, N. H. in 1844, and "formed a church with three male and six female members" : also preached in Linebrook parish in Ipswich, Mass. and in other places, being employed a part of the time by the New Hampshire Home Missionary Society. He however retained his residence in Windham until his death.

He prepared the following books or pamphlets, which were printed :—"Sermon delivered at the funeral of Miss Mary Colby of Auburn, N. H., Dec. 11, 1815 : to which are added extracts from some of her writings, and an account of her last sickness and death "[‡] This was printed at Exeter, N. H., in 1816.—"Memoirs of Miss Mary Campbell of Windham, who died July 21, 1819"[§] : printed in 1820 at Haverhill, Mass.—"Questions on Christian Experience and Character."[§] This consists of about eighty questions with

<hr>

[*] Rev. Loren Thayer in the "History of New Hampshire Churches."
[†] Rev. Samuel Harris' once made the journey from Windham, N. H. to Philadelphia, Pa. *on horseback*—probably to attend a meeting of the General Assembly of the Presbyterian Church.
[‡] Miss Harriet Dinsmoor of Windham, N. H., has a copy of this book.
[§] W. S. Harris' of Windham, has copies of these books.

Sally Harris.

Edward P. Harris.

Mrs. Ruth P. Harris.

John M. Harris.

William C. Harris.

answers selected from the Scriptures. Two editions were issued: printed at Newburyport, Mass. in 1827, and at Haverhill, Mass. in 1828.—His Farewell Sermon, occasioned by his dismission from the church in Windham was also printed. Of his ten children who lived to maturity all taught school more or less except one, Samuel[6].

The accompanying group of portraits includes his wife, Mrs. Ruth-Pratt Harris, and six of their children.

Samuel Harris[5] married, April 17, 1798, Ruth Pratt, daughter of Edward and Ruth (Pool) Pratt. Her mother married, 2, Dea. Jacob Harris[4] [see No. 17.]. She was born in New Ipswich, N. H., August 29, 1779; died in Windham, N. H., March 22, 1869, aged 89½.

CHILDREN.

34. Sally   [59]. b. Feb. 20, 1799, in Fitchburg, Mass.
35. Mary-Winchester   , b. Nov. 3, 1800, in F. d. Jan. 18, 1839, in W.
36. Edward-Pratt   [60]. b. Nov. 17, 1802, d. March 19, 1868.
37. Samuel   [63]. b. Dec. 7, 1804, d. May 6, 1860.
38. John-Milton   [71]. b. Oct. 18, 1806, d. July 26, 1877.
39. Jacob   [74]. b. Sept. 30, 1809, d. July 5, 1861.
40. Lydia-Kimball [76]. b. Feb. 21, 1813, d. Aug. 18, 1852.
41. William   , b. March 19, 1815, d. Oct. 5, 1817.
42. Elizabeth   [77]. b. March 5, 1817, d. Sept. 22, 1853.
43. Luther   [79]. b. Sept. 11, 1820, d. Oct. 1, 1841.
44. William-Calvin [80]. b. Dec. 14, 1822.
45. Lucinda   , b. June 10, 1824, d. April 27, 1825.

46. MARTHA[5] [22.] (Dea. Jacob[4], Richard[3], Serjt. John[2], John[1]), married, August 8, 1808, JOSHUA MOORE, a farmer, third son of John and Esther Moore. He was born in Worcester, Mass., Nov. 20, 1773, and died in Westminster, Mass., May 17, 1848. He married, 1, May, 1799, Deborah Townsend of Athol, Mass., by whom he had three children*: she died April 7, 1806, aged 26 years, 6 months; he married,

*The children of Joshua and Deborah (Townsend) Moore were:—
1. Eliza, b. April 27, 1800, m. June 16, 1839, Constant Southworth, lives in South Gardner, Mass.
2. Arad, b. March 13, 1802, m. Sept., 1843, Mrs. Harriet Maynard, d. Jan. 5, 1869; left one son.
3. Emily, b. Aug. 26, 1804, d. April 3, 1806.

2. Martha Harris⁵. They lived in Westminster; she lived
the last years of her life and died in Gardner. Mass.

CHILDREN, BORN IN WESTMINSTER, MASS.

47. Emily   , b. March 18, 1810, d. Nov. 8, 1881, in Framing-
                                   ham, Mass.
48. Marius-Harris   [84], b. May 21, 1814.
49. Cordelia-Esther   [88], b. Aug. 21, 1823.
50. John-Milton   [91], b. July 22, 1827.

51. Jacob⁵, Junior [23] (Dea. Jacob⁴, Richard³, Serjt.
John², John¹), was a farmer; settled on his father's homestead
in Ashburnham, Mass., where he lived until the spring of
1826; then removed to Windham, N. H.; lived many years
on a farm on the slopes of "Jenny's hill", then sold and
bought the homestead one-half mile north of Windham Center where he died, and where his widow and sister Eunice⁵
also died. He joined the Congregational church in Ashburnham in 1826; was made a Ruling Elder in the Presbyterian church in Windham, Jan. 10, 1833. He was at one
time a member of the School Committee of Windham. He
was a hard-working man; was strictly honest, and much respected; was a close student of the Bible, and very useful in
the Sabbath school. He married, April 8, 1817, Sophy
Smith*, who was born in 1787, and died April 23, 1869, aged
81 years and 6 months. She joined the church in Ashburnham in 1816.

52. Eunice⁵ [24] (Dea. Jacob⁴, Richard³, Serjt. John²
John¹), lived at home with her father and brother Jacob⁵ in
Ashburnham, and removed with them in 1826, to Windham.
N. H., where she died, June 18, 1877, aged over 87. She
retained a clear memory in regard to dates and facts concerning the history of the family. The origin of this work depended largely on information given by her, respecting her
grandfather's family.

*W.-S. Harris¹ of Windham, N. H. has cups and saucers which belonged
to the wedding set of Sophy Smith and Jacob Harris⁵, Jr., married in 1817.
He has also a cup and saucer of more ancient style which belonged to Sophy
Smith's mother.

SIXTH GENERATION.

53. JACOB-HARRIS MERRIAM[6] [26.] (Betsy[5] (Merriam),
Dea. Jacob[4], Richard[3], Serjt. John[2], John[1]), studied two
years, commencing in 1822, at Appleton Academy, New
Ipswich, N. H.; then entered the Congregational Theological Seminary at Bangor, Me. in 1824, and completed the
regular course of three years, graduating in 1827. He was
licensed to preach for three years by a Congregational Association at Bangor, and afterwards preached a few years,
but changed his plans and was never ordained to the ministry.
He turned his attention to agriculture and has resided in
Fitchburg, Mass. since his marriage. His age (March, 1883)
is 84. He married, Nov. 27, 1834, Abigail-Lowe Wheeler.

CHILDREN, BORN IN FITCHBURG, MASS.

54.   Mary-Elizabeth, b. Jan. 4, 1838; is a dress-maker; resides with her parents.
55.   Sarah-Abbie, b. Sept. 24, 1839, d. Nov. 26, 1855, in Fitchburg.
56.   Ellen-Augusta [96], b. Sept. 21, 1840, d. Dec. 12, 1874.
57.   Lyman-Wheeler [98], b. March 31, 1844.

58. BETSEY MERRIAM[6] [32.] (Betsy[5] (Merriam), Dea.
Jacob[4], Richard[3], Serjt. John[2], John[1]), married, June 10,
1841, JOHN-MILTON HARRIS[6]. See Nos. 38, 71, for an
account of him and of their children.

59. SALLY[6] [34.] (Rev. Samuel[5], Dea. Jacob[4], Richard[3],
Serjt. John[2], John[1]), married, Oct. 19, 1852, AMHERST COULT
of Auburn, N. H., a farmer, son of Dr. Amherst and Miriam
(Giddings) Coult. He was born in Lyme, N. H. May 17,
1797; married, 1, Feb. 8, 1831, Anna, daughter of Benjamin-
P. and Mary Chase, of Auburn, who died July 1, 1852.
They had several children, the youngest of whom, Frank-B.,
lives on the homestead with his father. He married, 2,
Sally Harris[6]. The oldest of the large family of Rev.
Samuel Harris[5], she has outlived all but William-Calvin[6],
and now (March, 1883) lives with her husband on the old
Chester Turnpike in Auburn. Their ages are 84 and 85.
(See group of portraits). (See No. 133).

60.   EDWARD-PRATT⁶ [36.] (Rev. Samuel⁵, Dea. Jacob⁴, Richard³, Serjt. John², John¹), was born in Ashburnham, Mass. and died in Rochester, Mich.   He fitted for college at Phillips Academy in Exeter, N. H. and at Atkinson, N. H. Academy; graduated at Dartmouth College in 1826.* He then was principal of the Academy at Bradford, Vt. and of Chesterfield, N. H. Academy, being at the latter place in 1827 and 1828.   He studied law with H.-F. Everritt of Hartford, Vt. ; practiced law several years at White River Junction village in Hartford, Vt. ; removed to Michigan in 1836 ; settled in Rochester village in Avon township, Oakland County, and practiced law there until his death.   He was Postmaster of Rochester in President Fillmore's term ; was Circuit Court Commissioner for Oakland County two terms, 1859-60, and 1861-62, elected by the people ; and was a Delegate to the Convention to revise the State Constitution in 1867.   (See group of portraits.)   He married, 1, June 29, 1829, Eliza Wright, daughter of David Wright of Hartford. She died in Hartford, Sept. 1, 1834.

CHILD, BORN IN HARTFORD, VT.

61.   Edward-Wright [106], b. May 4, 1834.

He married, 2, Dec. 3, 1835, Elizabeth-Sanborn Gillet, daughter of Israel Gillet of Hartford.   She died April 23, 1877, aged 76.

CHILD, BORN IN HARTFORD, VT.

62.   Samuel [115], b. Sept. 15, 1836.

63   SAMUEL⁶ [37.] (Rev. Samuel⁵, Dea. Jacob⁴, Richard³, Serjt. John², John¹), was born in Ashburnham, Mass. and died in Melrose, Mass.   At the age of fifteen he went to Haverhill, Mass. to learn the printer's trade.   A letter of recommendation dated Haverhill, March 25, 1826, and signed by Isaac-R. How states that Samuel Harris⁶ had been an apprentice in the office of the *Gazette and Patriot* when

---

*He received the degree of Master of Arts in course, probably three years after graduation.

owned by Nathan Burrill, of whom Mr. How bought the establishment in Feb., 1824. Mr. Harris worked the last two years of his apprenticeship under Mr. How. Then (probably in the spring of 1826) he went to Lowell, Mass. and worked for a Mr. Knowlton some years. Then went to Boston, worked in the type foundry first, afterwards went into business with George Light in printing and publishing. After that he worked for John-B. Hall, and then went into business with Mr. Wier, and continued in partnership with him until death. He removed to Melrose from Boston in the fall of 1848; was one of the early members of the Congregational church in Melrose, and of great activity and usefulness in the church ; was Superintendent of the Sabbath school, and afterwards teacher of a Bible class. He had great knowledge of the Scriptures, and was a man of excellent Christian character, and much respected. (See group of portraits.) He married, Jan. 16, 1832, Mary Hall of Boston, who still lives in Melrose, Mass.

CHILDREN, BORN IN BOSTON, MASS.

64. Eliza-Hall   [120]. b. Oct. 20, 1832, d. July 19, 1873.
65. Mary-Harriet   , b. Oct. 20, 1835, d. April 15, 1839.
66. Edward-Payson   , b. Feb., 1840, d. Sept. 10, 1843.
67. Samuel-Austin   , b. Nov., 1842, d. Sept. 1, 1843.
68. George-Wheeler   [122]. b. July 21, 1844.
69. John-William   , b. Oct. 16, 1846; lives in Melrose: is a manufacturer of gentlemen's neckties.
70. Charles-Samuel   , b. Sept., 1848, d. Nov. 20, 1851.

71. JOHN-MILTON[6] [38.] (Rev. Samuel[5], Dea. Jacob[4], Richard[3], Serjt. John[2], John[1]), was born in Windham, N. H. at "Jenny's hill", and died in Fitchburg, Mass. All his younger brothers and sisters were born in Windham. His son Edwin-A. Harris[7] writes of him :—"He served an apprenticeship of three years at Derry, N. H. in learning the carpenter's trade, and subsequently lived in Rowley and Georgetown, Mass. After attaining his majority he prepared for college at Phillips Academy in Andover, Mass. and at Amherst, Mass. Academy, studying at the latter place

a year. He entered Amherst College in 1835, working his own way through, intending to enter the Christian ministry. During the last year of college experience the severity of his labors told upon his physical health and he was obliged to relinquish the greater part of his studies. He graduated however with the class of 1839. Among his classmates were Bishop F.-D. Huntington of Central New York and Rev. Dr. R.-S. Storrs of Brooklyn, N. Y. Two years after graduation he married and settled in Nashua, N. H. where he remained until 1843, when he bought and removed to the farm on which he died in Fitchburg.

"In his business relations he was a man of strict integrity, esteeming highly the confidence of his fellow men, and governed wholly in his dealings by the law of Christian love. In his religious belief he was strong in the conviction of the truth of Evangelical doctrines. In his social character he was a man of pure heart, of generous impulses, affectionate, companionable—pre-eminently the one to whom his neighbors resorted in times of trouble and affliction. He was a model Sabbath school teacher, always punctually at his post, a careful Bible student, a clear and logical reasoner, a thorough Christian."

He was elected Deacon of the Calvinistic Congregational church in Fitchburg, Feb. 27, 1863, and was dismissed from the office by removal of membership in Dec., 1875. He was Superintendent of the Sabbath school for some time. On the day of his funeral, Sunday, July 29, 1877, his youngest grandchild John-Milton Harris', [see No. 131.] was baptized. (See group of portraits.) He married, June 10, 1841, Betsey Merriam' of Fitchburg [see Nos. 32, 58.], who lives with her younger son on the homestead in Fitchburg.

CHILDREN.

72. Edwin-Augustine, [25 .b. April 8, 1842.
73. Charles-Cornelius   b. July 11, 1846, in Fitchburg, Mass. He has been reporter for the Fitchburg daily and weekly *Sentinel* since Oct. 24, 1876.

74. JACOB⁶ [39.] (Rev. Samuel⁵, Dea. Jacob⁴, Richard³, Serjt. John², John¹), was born in Windham, and died in Concord, N. H. He prepared for college at Phillips Academy, Andover, Mass., intending to go through college and fit himself for the life and labors of a foreign missionary of the Gospel. But his health failed and he was obliged to give up further study. He lived in Windham, N. H., and was a member of the Superintending School Committee for many years. He was a man of intelligence and of upright character, and had the respect of all who knew him. (See group of portraits.) He married, June 10, 1852, Rufina Merrill, daughter of Amos and Mehitable (Smith) Merrill, born in Windham, April 12, 1816; she lives with her daughter in Windham.

CHILD, BORN IN WINDHAM, N. H.

75. Charlotte-Elizabeth, b. April 3, 1855; has been a school-teacher since the spring of 1872.

76. LYDIA-KIMBALL⁶ [40.] (Rev. Samuel⁵, Dea. Jacob⁴, Richard³, Serjt. John², John¹), married, Dec. 17, 1835, STEPHEN DEARBORN, a farmer, and lived on the Chester Turnpike in Auburn, N. H., where she died. He was born Aug. 10, 1796, and died March 16, 1859. He was a prominent man in town affairs ; was selectman, and Representative to the State Legislature. He married, 2, Mary-A. Craige, and had two children, Stephen, who died young, and Jennie, who married Charles Richardson and lives in Manchester, N. H.

77. ELIZABETH⁶ [42.] (Rev. Samuel⁵, Dea. Jacob⁴, Richard³, Serjt. John², John¹), married, March 20, 1849, JAMES UNDERHILL, a farmer, and lived in Auburn, N. H., where she died. He was the son of James and Elizabeth (Chase) Underhill, born Feb. 20, 1822. In June, 1854 he removed to Ohio, and now resides in Richfield, Summit Co., Ohio. He married, 2, April 15, 1857, Mrs. Ann Bassett, widow of John-W. Bassett, whose daughter Mary-J. married

George-Calvin Underhill[5] [see Nos. 78, 133]. James and Elizabeth (Harris[6]) Underhill had one

CHILD, BORN IN AUBURN, N. H.

78.   George-Calvin [133], b. March 1, 1852.

79.   LUTHER[6] [45.] (Rev. Samuel[5], Dea. Jacob[4], Richard[3], Serjt. John[2], John[1]), received a good education at Hancock, N. H., Academy, and taught district schools in Pelham and Roxbury, N. H., and in the fall of 1841 he opened a private high school in Marlborough, N. H.   This was attended by forty scholars, coming from six towns.   He had classes in Astronomy, Philosophy, Algebra, Surveying, Latin Reader, etc.   He was a fine scholar, and intended to fit himself for the lawyer's profession, but his life, so full of promise for a useful and brilliant future, terminated suddenly and sadly at Marlborough, at the age of 21.

80.   WILLIAM-CALVIN[6] [44.] (Rev. Samuel[5], Dea. Jacob[4], Richard[3], Serjt. John[2], John[1]), was born, and still resides, on the homestead in Windham, N. H., which his father bought and cleared up from woodland, and in the house which was built in 1811.   He is a farmer; has been a Justice of the Peace for many years; represented his native town in the New Hampshire Legislature of 1865; and has at various times held nearly all the town offices; was moderator many years, town clerk, first selectman, treasurer, first supervisor, etc.   He was made a Ruling Elder in the Presbyterian church in Windham, Dec. 26, 1878, and has been Superintendent of the Sabbath school since April, 1878; previously was a teacher in the Sabbath school.   (See group of portraits.)   He married, June 23, 1853, Philena-Heald Dinsmore*, daughter

* She descended from David Dinsmore,[3] whose grandfather John went from Scotland to Ireland.   David[1] sailed from Londonderry, Ireland, to America about 1745; bought a farm and settled in Auburn, N. H., in 1747.   His son Robert[2], born in Auburn, March 24, 1752, succeeded him on the homestead, and was succeeded by his son Dea. Samuel, born Feb. 15, 1788, died March 1, 1861; he married, Dec. 26, 1811, Hannah, daughter of Joseph Blanchard, Esq., born Jan. 6, 1790, died May 16, 1871; they celebrated their Golden Wedding in 1861; had twelve children; the eleventh was Philena-Heald[4], born on the old family homestead Oct. 3, 1831. [see No. 80.].

of Dea. Samuel and Hannah (Blanchard) Dinsmore of Auburn, N. H., born in Auburn, (then Chester,) Oct. 3, 1831. They celebrated their Silver Wedding in 1878.

CHILDREN, BORN IN WINDHAM, N. H.

81.   Albert-Miles, b. June 9, 1857, d. Dec. 12, 1875, in Windham.
82.   William-Samuel [136.], b. March 29, 1861; author of this History.
83.   Mary-Ella, b. April 19, 1866.

84.   MARIUS-HARRIS MOORE[5] [48.] (Martha[3] (Moore), Dea. Jacob[4], Richard[3], Serjt. John[2], John[1]), is a mechanic, as are his two sons; they live in Leominster, Mass. He married, August 26, 1847, Elizabeth Wood, daughter of James and Maria (Butler) Wood, born in Leominster, Mass., March 20, 1822. They celebrated their Silver Wedding in 1872.

CHILDREN.

85.   William-Everett, b. June 20, 1852, in Leominster, Mass.
86.   Wilbur-Francis, b. June 25, 1860, in Westminster, Mass.
87.   Emma-Cordelia, b. Oct. 1, 1864, in Westminster, Mass.

88.   CORDELIA-ESTHER MOORE[5] [49.] (Martha[3] (Moore), Dea. Jacob[4], Richard[3], Serjt. John[2], John[1]), married, Nov. 8, 1849, FRANKLIN-HARVEY SPRAGUE, a farmer, son of William and Anne Sprague, born May 19, 1825, in Phillipston, Mass. They lived in Boston; removed to Framingham, Mass., in Sept., 1865, where they now reside. He was a member of the Massachusetts Legislature from Boston in 1858 and from Framingham in 1873 and 1874; was selectman in Framingham six years, and a member of the School Board nine years. They celebrated their Silver Wedding in 1874.

CHILDREN.

89.   Mary-Cordelia [137.], b. Jan. 4, 1851, in Boston, Mass.
90.   Anna-Maria, b. May 24, 1855, in Boston; is a school-teacher in Framingham.
91.   Hattie-Elizabeth, b. June 27, 1857, in Boston; lives with her parents.
92.   Edward-Franklin, b. April 18, 1861, in Boston; is engaged in trade in Framingham.
93.   Myra-Moore, b. July 27, 1865, in Waltham, Mass.

94.   JOHN-MILTON MOORE[5] [50.] (Martha[3] (Moore), Dea. Jacob[4], Richard[3], Serjt. John[2], John[1]), lives in South Gard-

ner, Mass. He was a member of the School Committee of Gardner for twenty-three years ending March, 1881, and has been a Justice of the Peace for twenty-eight years. He represented the town of Gardner in the Massachusetts Legislature in 1855, being the youngest member of the House. He was again a member in 1870, representing the district of which Gardner forms a part. He was one of a Committee of three chosen by the town to publish a History of Gardner in 1878. In Nov., 1880 he was elected State Senator from the Fourth Worcester Senatorial District of Massachusetts for the term of one year commencing Jan., 1881. The district is territorially the largest in the State and includes seventeen towns :—Athol, Barre, Dana, Gardner, Hardwick, Holden, Hubbardston, New Braintree, North Brookfield, Oakham, Paxton, Petersham, Phillipston, Royalston, Rutland, Templeton, and Winchendon, having a population in 1880 of 35,500. In the special session which completed the revision of the Public Statutes he was chairman of an important Committee. In Nov., 1881 he was re-elected to the Senate for the term of 1882. In this Legislature he was appointed chairman of the Senate Committee on Education. He married, Nov. 29, 1854, Myra-Allen Sawin, daughter of Joseph-D. and Marcia-M. (Scribner) Sawin, born in Gardner, July 12, 1832.

CHILD, BORN IN GARDNER, MASS.

95. John-Myron, b. Nov. 3, 1866.

SEVENTH GENERATION.

96. ELLEN-AUGUSTA MERRIAM[7] [56.] (Jacob-Harris Merriam[6], Betsy[5] (Merriam), Dea. Jacob[4], Richard[3], Serjt. John[2], John[1]), married, Oct. 27, 1870, CHARLES-B. PRESCOTT, son of Abram-Tilton Prescott, a carriage-maker, and lived in Pittsfield, N. H., where she died. He now resides in Milford, Mass.

CHILD, BORN IN PITTSFIELD, N. H.

97. George-Tilton, b. Dec. 8, 1871.

98. LYMAN-WHEELER MERRIAM[7] [57.] (Jacob-Harris Merriam[6], Betsy[5] (Merriam), Dea. Jacob[4], Richard[3], Serjt. John[2], John[1]), is a mechanic and lives in Winchendon, Mass. He has obtained three patents for mechanical inventions, two of them shingling brackets and one a slating bracket, which are said to be the best roof brackets ever invented. In company with John Hancock of Winchendon he is engaged in the manufacture of an improved style of window-blind hinges and fastenings, also slaters' brackets. He married, July 16, 1868, Ellen-Maria Lowe, daughter of John and Sarah (Meade) Lowe, born in Fitchburg, Mass., April 30, 1847.

CHILDREN.

99. Sarah-Abbie, b. Aug. 9, 1869, in Fitchburg, Mass.
100. Frederic-Lowe, b. Aug. 2, 1871, in Fitchburg; d. April 23, 1872, in Worcester, Mass.
101. Louisa-Adeline, b. Aug. 21, 1872, in Holden, Mass.
102. Alice-Edna, b. Nov. 25, 1874, in Fitchburg, Mass.
103. John-Lowe, b. July 9, 1876, in Jaffrey, N. H.
104. Edith-Augusta, b. March 5, 1878, in Jaffrey, N. H.
105. Lizzie-Maria, b. Sept. 27, 1880, in Winchendon, Mass.

106. EDWARD-WRIGHT[7] [61.] (Edward-Pratt[6], Rev. Samuel[5], Dea. Jacob[4], Richard[3], Serjt. John[2], John[1]). He attended the Academy at Romeo, Mich., about three months in 1850; commenced the study of law with his father Edward-Pratt Harris[6] [see No. 60.] at Rochester, Mich., about 1851. In the fall of 1853 he attended the State and National Law School at Poughkeepsie, N. Y., one term, and in the following winter spent three or four months in the office of Daniel and David-J. Clark at Manchester, N. H. In the spring of 1854 he returned to Poughkeepsie, was there one term and graduated. He was admitted to the bar in the fall of 1854, and in December went to Port Huron, Mich., to live, where he has since resided. In June, 1855 he went into partnership with Omer-D. Conger, Esq.; they practiced law together until Mr. Conger was elected Representative to Congress in the fall of 1868. He is now a United States Senator from Michigan, having been elected for the term

commencing March 4, 1881. Mr. Harris continued the practice of law in Port Huron until January, 1873, when he was appointed Judge of the Sixteenth Judicial District (or 16th Circuit) of Michigan, which is composed of the counties of Macomb and St. Clair. In the spring of 1875 he was elected by the people for the term of six years without opposition.* His term of office as Judge expired with the close of the year 1881, and since that time he has practised law in partnership with Samuel-W. Vance, Esq. Judge Harris has a large, well-selected, and valuable library, particularly rich in works relating to Shakspeare.† He married, Oct. 1, 1857, Sarah-Jane Whitman, daughter of Randall and Sarah-Jane (Severance) Whitman, born August 30, 1837.

CHILDREN, BORN IN PORT HURON, MICH.

107.   Lillie-Eliza [139.], b. Sept. 11, 1858.
108.   Frances-Alma, b. April 5, 1860, d. Jan. 20, 1861.

---

* At the sixth annual banquet of the Port Huron Lotus Club, Nov. 18, 1880, a poem by Prof. Bigsby of Iowa was read, of which the following is one stanza :—

> "I see before me the judge,
>   His features lit up with a smile,
> As he deals out his witticisms,
> Kind, modest criticisms,
>   In a quiet and fatherly style ;
> As though in his dealings
> He might injure one's feelings
>   Like mythical Paris,
> Is he still the same gentle,
> Good-natured, parental,
>   Joke-loving JUDGE HARRIS ?
> Does he tell of the glories
>   Of Bad Axe, the beautiful ?
> Does he still tell the stories
>   Of counsellors dutiful ?
> Is his laugh just as ready,
>   His jest just as free ?
> Does he still woo each lady
>   With innocent glee ?
> Does he still let the Ay's
>   Of the fair sex count double,
> While the No's of the men-folk
>   Get snubbed into trouble ?"

† He has in his possession a silver-headed cane which was originally owned by John-B. Hall of Boston, Mass., brother of Mary Hall [see No. 63.]; it was owned and used by Rev. Samuel Harris, grandfather of the present owner, and Edward-P. Harris, his father.

109.   Eloise-Wright, b. Sept. 19, 1861, d. Dec. 2, 1861,
110.   Mary-Jane, b. Aug. 21, 1863, d. Sept. 10, 1863,
111.   Willie, b. Aug. 22, 1865, d. Sept. 15, 1865,
112.   William-Edward, b. Dec. 8, 1866, d. Aug. 15, 1867,
113.   May, b. May 8, 1868, d. Aug. 11, 1868,
114.   Kittie-Wright, b. Feb. 9, 1871.

115.   SAMUEL[7] [62.] (Edward-Pratt[6], Rev. Samuel[5], Dea.
Jacob[4], Richard[3], Serjt. John[2], John[1]).   He was at Rochester, Mich. when the Civil war broke out, running a machine-
shop and foundry.   He enlisted August, 1862, in Co. A, 5th
Regiment Michigan Volunteer Cavalry, and was at once
elected Second Lieutenant.   He was in several small engage-
ments in the winter and spring of 1863; was in the four
days' fight at Gettysburg in July; was on picket duty most of
the succeeding fall and winter.   In Feb., 1864, he was de-
tailed to take command of Company F, 5th Michigan Cavalry, and to report with his company to Col. Ulrich Dahlgren
at Stevensburg, Va.   The Secretary of War had ordered a
charge to be made on Richmond to liberate the Union pris-
oners in Libby and other prisons.   Col. Dahlgren was to go
with a detachment of 400 men to act in co-operation with another detachment under Gen. Kilpatrick.   They crossed the
Rapidan river, capturing the pickets at the ford, flanked
Lee's army, and marched towards Richmond, where they
were to meet Gen. Kilpatrick, but by the treachery of their
guide were led fifty miles out of their course, up the James
river.

When they reached Goochland, twenty miles above Richmond, the country seat of Gen. Seddon, the Confederate Secretary of State, a part of the command burned a large flour-
mill and demolished the rich and costly furniture in the fine
large residence.   This was done, however, not by any men
under command of Capt. Harris nor by any of his regiment.
From there they marched on towards Richmond.   A little
out of the city they met about 1,000 men of the Confederate
Home Guard, and in charging them Capt. Harris was badly
wounded in the left shoulder.   Being weak from loss of blood

he was captured the next day, and was taken to the Capital Square in Richmond, where he was kept over two hours while a scaffold was being prepared to hang him upon, it being reported that Gen. Seddon had ordered his execution. Not less than 10,000 people came to see him there. That afternoon President Davis called a meeting of his Cabinet, and every member voted for hanging him. Davis, however, thought this inexpedient, and he was taken to Libby prison and placed in the hospital. This was on March 4, 1864. He staid in Libby prison two months, enduring great suffering, and was then taken successively to Danville, Va., Macon and Savannah, Ga., Charleston and Columbia, S. C., then back to Charleston, and there exchanged, after having been in prison over nine months; and he received his discharge April 14, 1865.

He has invented an improved style of stationary engine; resides at present in Chicago, Ill., and is a dealer in machinists' supplies. He married, 1, May 28, 1858, Sarah-H. Richardson of Rochester, Mich., born May 8, 1841, died Nov. 2, 1871.

CHILDREN.

116. Frances-Adelia, b. June 10, 1860, d. April 9, 1862.
117. Charles-Sumner, b. Feb. 28, 1866, in Washington, D. C.
118. Edward-Palen, b. Sept. 29, 1870, d. Feb. 1, 1871.

He married, 2, Nov. 25, 1872, Sarah-S. Ladd, born May 11, 1852.

CHILD, BORN IN CHICAGO, ILL.

119. Sarah-Elizabeth, b. June 20, 1874.

120. ELIZA-HALL[7] [64.] (Samuel[6], Rev. Samuel[5], Dea. Jacob[4], Richard[3], Serjt. John[2], John[1]), married, April 8, 1860, FARWELL-BROWN PEAKES, son of Benjamin-Horton and Maria (Moore) Peakes, born in Fairfield, Me., Feb. 3, 1827; they lived in Boston; removed in the spring of 1870 to a farm in Saugus, Mass., where she died. He lives at present in Melrose, Mass., and is a travelling dealer in gentlemen's neck-ties.

CHILD, BORN IN BOSTON, MASS.

121. Eliza-Georgietta, b. June 18, 1868.

122. GEORGE-WHEELER[7] [68.] (Samuel[6], Rev. Samuel[5], Dea. Jacob[4], Richard[3], Serjt. John[2], John[1]), resides in Melrose, Mass.; is book-keeper for Simons, Hatch & Whitten, Boston, Mass., wholesale dealers in gentlemen's furnishing goods; he is also engaged in the manufacture of gentlemen's neck-ties. He married, May 15, 1869, Mattie-Louisa Handlen.

CHILDREN.

123. Frank-Tucker, b. July 24, 1871, in New York, N. Y.
124. George-Wheeler, b. Sept. 24, 1880, in Melrose, Mass.
124½. Son, b. March 30, 1883, in Melrose, Mass.

125. EDWIN-AUGUSTINE[7] [72.] (Dea. John-Milton[6], Rev. Samuel[5], Dea. Jacob[4], Richard[3], Serjt. John[2], John[1]: also Betsey Merriam[6] (Harris), Betsy[5] (Merriam), Dea. Jacob[4], etc.). He was born in Nashua, N. H., and resides in Fitchburg, Mass. He was in the Civil war: enlisted August 24, 1862, in Co. A, 53rd Regiment Massachusetts Volunteers: served in the Department of the Gulf under Gen. Banks in New Orleans and western Louisiana: was not wounded but suffered much from sickness: was honorably discharged at the expiration of the term of service, Sept. 2, 1863. He has been in Railroad service since 1864: was Baggage Master of the first passenger train that ever ran over the Boston, Clinton & Fitchburg Railroad between Fitchburg and Boston, July 2, 1866: was Conductor of the first passenger train that ever ran over the Framingham & Lowell Railroad: is at present a Conductor on the Old Colony Railroad, Northern Division.

He is the author of "A Hero of Fitchburg: Asa Thurston", a sketch of the life of Rev. Asa Thurston, one of the pioneer missionaries of the "American Board" to the Sandwich Islands in 1820. This was printed as a pamphlet of twenty-four pages,—illustrated by portraits of Mr. and Mrs. Thurston—in Fitchburg, Mass., in May, 1878. He is a contributor to the *Congregationalist* (Boston), the Boston daily *Journal*, Fitchburg *Sentinel*, and has also written for the Fitchburg *Reveille*, and other papers; and was newspaper reporter for a short time. His style of writing is graceful and pleasing. Accompanied by his brother Charles-C[5]. [see No. 73.], he spent the winter of 1874-5 in Florida for his health. In the autumn of 1875 he visited California for the same object. He has been a Justice of the Peace for several years, and is at present a member of the School Board of Fitchburg, elected for a term of three years, 1881-3. He was for two years Assistant Superintendent of the Sabbath school of the Rollstone Congregational church, having charge of the infant department; and is active in all religious work, particularly among railroad men; is an active member and officer of the Fitchburg Railroad Men's Christian Association. Accompanied by his wife he spent a portion of the winter of 1881-2 in Philadelphia and Baltimore in evangelistic work among railroad employes. They spent the succeeding winter engaged in the same work in Philadelphia, Cumberland, Md., Martinsburg and Parkersburg, W. Va., and other cities in that region. Good success attended their labors. Mrs. Harris *sings* the gospel with great beauty and effectiveness.

He married, Sept. 19, 1867, Emma-Mindwell Caswell, daughter of Samuel-M. and Elizabeth-L.-D. (Thurston)* Caswell of Fitchburg, born in Fitchburg, Sept. 6, 1849.

CHILDREN, BORN IN FITCHBURG, MASS.

126. Edward-Melville (140.), b. Aug. 10, 1868.
127. Annie-Gertrude-Thurston [see No. 140.], b. Dec. 1, 1869.
128. Charles-Herbert, b. March 18, 1871.
129. Frederic-Walter [see No. 140.], b. Sept. 1, 1872.
130. Bessie-Mabel, b. May 27, 1875, d. Sept. 7, 1876, in Fitchburg.
131. John-Milton [see No. 71.], b. Dec. 30, 1876.
132. Lester-Eugene, b. Oct. 11, 1878, d. May 21, 1880, in Fitchburg.

133. GEORGE-CALVIN UNDERHILL[7] [78.] (Elizabeth[6] (Underhill), Rev. Samuel[5], Dea. Jacob[4], Richard[3], Serjt. John[2], John[1]), lived with his aunt, Mrs. Sally Coult[6] [see No.

* Elizabeth-L.-D. Thurston's father, Ebenezer, was a brother to Rev. Asa Thurston, the missionary.

59.] in Auburn, N. H., from the time of his mother's death until the age of eighteen. He then went to Richfield, Ohio, where he lived until March, 1879, at that date removing to Unadilla, Otoe Co., Nebraska, where he now resides; is a farmer. See portrait of Mr. Underhill, here inserted. He married, Nov. 8, 1870, Mary-J. Bassett, daughter of John-W. and Ann Bassett [see No. 77.], born in Northfield, Summit Co., Ohio, Nov. 4, 1849.

CHILDREN.

134. Minnie-Ann, b. Oct. 3, 1871, in Richfield, Ohio.
135. George-Walter, b. May 31, 1881, in Unadilla, Neb.
135½. Son, b. April 2, 1883, in Unadilla, Neb.

136. WILLIAM-SAMUEL[7] [82.] (Dea. William-Calvin[6], Rev. Samuel[5], Dea. Jacob[4], Richard[4], Serjt. John[2], John[1]), the author of this History of the Harris Family, was born March 29, 1861, at the Harris homestead in Windham, N. H., and now resides there. He received a plain English education in the public schools of Windham and at Pinkerton Academy in Derry, N. H., being especially interested in the natural sciences and the departments of natural history; acquired a thorough and practical knowledge of Botany, and has collected a herbarium representing the flora of Windham containing nearly three hundred specimens. He has taught school in Windham, and has been since Feb., 1882, a teacher in the Presbyterian Sabbath school. Has been from early life fond of literary pursuits and has contributed to various periodicals since 1880; has written articles on a variety of subjects, descriptive, botanical, historical, and religious, which have been published in *The New York Evangelist*, *The Presbyterian* (Philadelphia), *Sabbath-School Visitor* (Philadelphia), *Massachusetts Ploughman* (Boston), Lowell, Mass. *Mail*, Manchester, N. H. *Mirror*, Exeter, N. H. *News-Letter*, and several other papers; has also been local news correspondent of the *News-Letter* since 1876. He furnished for the "History of Windham, N. H.", by Leonard A. Morrison (published in 1883), an account of the Harrises con-

nected with that town. He now (March, 1883) publishes this History of the Harris Family, for the preparation of which he has been gathering information for many years.

137. MARY-CORDELIA SPRAGUE[7] [89.] (Cordelia-Esther Moore[6] (Sprague), Martha[5] (Moore), Dea. Jacob[4], Richard[3], Serjt. John[2], John[1]), married, Sept. 14, 1871, CHAUNCEY-UPHAM FULLER, book-keeper and clerk ; they reside in Framingham, Mass.

CHILD, BORN in FRAMINGHAM, MASS.

138.   Franklin-Sprague, b. Nov. 17, 1876, d. May 3, 1878, in Framingham.

EIGHTH GENERATION.

139. LILLIE-ELIZA[8] [107.] (Edward-Wright[7], Edward-Pratt[6], Rev. Samuel[5], Dea. Jacob[4], Richard[3], Serjt. John[2], John[1]), graduated at the Port Huron high school, and at the State Normal School in Ypsilanti, Mich. in May, 1878, and has since been engaged in teaching in the public schools of Port Huron, Mich., living with her parents. Her ancestors in a direct line back to Dea. Jacob[4], each taught school more or less, making five successive generations of school teachers bearing the name of Harris.

140. EDWARD-MELVILLE[8] [126.] (Edwin-Augustine[7], Dea. John-Milton[6], Rev. Samuel[5], Dea. Jacob[4], Richard[3], Serjt. John[2], John[1] ; also Edwin-Augustine[7], Betsey Merriam[6] (Harris), Betsy[5] (Merriam), Dea. Jacob[4], etc.). He became a member of the Rollstone Congregational church in Fitchburg, Mass. March 6, 1881. He is the *sixth generation* [*] in direct descent—from Richard[3]—of male members of Orthodox Congregational churches in Massachusetts bearing the name of Harris. The same is true of his brother Frederic-W.[8] [see No. 129.], who, with their sister Annie-G.-T.[8] [see No. 127.], was admitted to the church at the same time. Thus in a remarkable manner is exemplified the truth that the

---

[*] Perhaps the *seventh*: Serjt. John[2], may have been a member of the church, as it appears from his will that he was a believer in Christ, and his son Richard[3] was baptized in infancy.

righteousness of the Lord is "unto children's children." "The just man walketh in his integrity: his children are blessed after him." "He is faithful that promised" to be "a God unto thee and to thy seed after thee." Spiritual, no less than physical and intellectual, tendencies and characteristics are transmitted to posterity, and a godly ancestry is better than inherited riches.

CHAPTER VII.

FOURTH GENERATION.—RICHARD HARRIS, JUNIOR.—HIS DE-
SCENDANTS.

141.   RICHARD HARRIS[4], JUNIOR [6.] (Richard[3], Serjt.
John[2], John[1]), was born in Ipswich, Mass.; baptized there
April 3, 1743.   His father the same year removed to Harvard, Mass.; in that town the son lived, and died there June
27, 1798, aged 55.   The homestead and farm—of about one
hundred acres—where he lived and died, was undoubtedly the
same where his father Richard[3] settled and lived [see No. 1.].
It is situated one mile from Harvard Center, midway between
that and Still River village, and is now owned and occupied
by H. Butterfield. The house is on elevated land with a wide
space in front, a most beautiful situation commanding an exten-
sive prospect, which includes Bear Hill pond, a sheet of water
of very rare beauty, dotted with islands.   Around the house
are some venerable trees which were set out by Richard[3], Jr.
The house has been much altered, but in the back part are
two or three rooms in their original condition.   The stairs are
the same, and the door-stone at the back entrance is the same
over which the feet of three generations of the Harris family
passed—placed there by Richard[3].

   Richard[3], Jr. was a carpenter, and "built the meeting-
house at Harvard, one at Littleton, one at Ipswich, and sev-

---

* "It is remembered that the wife of Richard[3], Jr. used to go out upon the
rocks across the road from the house, and make her voice heard by her boys
when they were fishing on the pond, and she wanted them to come home."

eral towards Worcester. At the time of the fight at Lexington, he was building a meeting-house at Boxborough." "He
was an upright, worthy man, and was held in high estimation
by his townsmen. There are quite a number of letters in exis-
tence written to his oldest son*, which show him to have been a
man of superior mind, a good penman and a ready writer, who
expressed himself in clear, easy style, a man greatly interested in the education of his children, and very fond of his
family." Richard Harris[4], Jr. and Lydia his wife joined the
Congregational church in Harvard, Dec. 17, 1769. He was
made Deacon (or "Elder") of the church Nov. 27, 1775, re-
taining the office until death. He was elected town clerk
and first selectman—holding both offices—for several years
ending in 1785; was also one of the selectmen in 1794-5-6-7.
He married Lydia Atherton of Harvard, who was baptized
Oct. 30, 1747, and died in Harvard, May 11, 1801. She
was the fourth and youngest daughter of John and Phebe
(Wright) Atherton of Harvard. Phebe married, 2. Richard
Harris[3], [see No. 1.]. Lois Atherton, sister to Lydia, married Grover Scollay [see No. 229.]. Richard[4], Jr. and Lydia had the following

CHILDREN, BORN IN HARVARD, MASS.

112. John [149.], b. Oct. 13, 1769, bapt. Dec. 17, 1769, d. April 23, 1845.
143. Asenath [154.], bapt. Aug. 30, 1772, d. March 22, 1800.
144. Lydia, b. May 15, 1775, bapt. May 21, 1775, d. Sept. 3, 1778, in Harvard.
145. Richard, bapt. Nov. 28, 1779, d. Oct. 3, 1784, in Harvard.
146. Joel [157.], bapt. Sept. 29, 1782, d. Dec. 2, 1817.
147. Sally or Sarah, bapt. Oct. 16, 1785; was a communicant in the Episco-
         pal church in Hopkinton, N. H., June 27, 1819; d. in Hopkinton
         between 1830 and 1840.
148. Harrison-Gray [163.], b. July 2, 1790, bapt. July 5, 1790, d. March 8,
         1875.

FIFTH GENERATION.

149. JOHN[5] [142.] (Dea. Richard[4], Jr., Richard[3], Serjt.
John[2], John[1]), was born in Harvard, Mass. and died in Hop-

---

* These letters are now in the possession of Misses A.-B. and M.-B. Harris[6] of Warner, N. H.

kinton, N. H.   He graduated at Harvard College in 1791;
was called "Jack Harris, very sedate, steady man in college."
"July 28, 1791, he entered the office of Hon. Simeon Strong
of Amherst, Mass., as a law student, where he acted as
clerk, and taught school also (probably a select school), and
showing the utmost diligence, as is proved by the certificate
sent by Judge Strong to Hon. Timothy Bigelow of Groton,
Mass., with whom he completed his law studies.   Judge
Strong says, "I can freely say that in my opinion his industry, application, and ingenuity were such that he progressed
as far in the time of his keeping school as might have been
expected from one who had attended wholly to the office." He
left the office of Mr. Bigelow in 1794, was admitted to the
bar, and commenced the practice of law in Hopkinton, N. H.
towards the close of the same year.

"In Nov., 1810 he was appointed Captain of the 4th Co. in
the 21st Regiment New Hampshire militia; resigned Sept.
23, 1812.   He was the first postmaster of Hopkinton, appointed Dec. 28, 1810; he resigned Aug. 1, 1821 and was
succeeded by his son.   He was Solicitor from 1817 to 1823;
Judge of Probate for Hillsborough County from Aug. 10,
1812 to 1823; also for Merrimack County from 1823, the
year of its formation, until 1843.   June 25, 1844, he was
chairman of a Committee "to designate the most eligible site
for a State House, and to prepare a plan for the same, to receive proposals for building, etc."   Dec. 19, 1816, a Trustee
of Dartmouth College; Dec. 23, 1820, chairman of a Committee to revise the Probate Laws of New Hampshire—by
request of the Legislature.   In Oct., 1816 Gov. Plumer appointed Judge Harris Associate Justice of the Supreme Court
of New Hampshire, but he declined the position.   In 1823 he
was again appointed to the office and accepted, holding it
from Oct. 6, 1823 to Jan. 5, 1833."

"Hon. John Harris in civil life was a distinguished jurist;
while in the Masonic world he was a star of great brilliancy.
He was the founder of Tyrean Council, and of Trinity

Chapter at Hopkinton nineteen years before. He was also the founder of Mount Horeb Commandery of Knights Templar of Hopkinton in 1826. It still further appears that he was Grand Master of the Grand Lodge, Grand High Priest of the Grand Chapter at its formation in 1819, and also first Grand Master of the Grand Encampment of Knights Templars of New Hampshire at its formation in 1826. The record of John Harris emblazons one of the most illustrious pages in the Masonic history of the United States".[*] He was a zealous Episcopalian, and one of the founders and prominent supporters of the Protestant Episcopal church in Hopkinton: his name is on a list of communicants in "Christ's Church," (Episcopal) Sept., 1816: his wife Mary-P. Harris was confirmed or admitted Aug. 20, 1817: their four children were baptized June 25, 1815. A new organization was formed, incorporated in 1827 "under the name of St. Andrew's Church. The first wardens were John Harris and William Little." He was one of a Committee to appraise the pews in the new church edifice in 1828, and owned shares in the building to the amount of $612.

"He was very methodical and everything relating to his affairs, his correspondence, etc., was kept in the nicest manner. He was very fond of gardening: indeed a reverence for trees and a love for things growing seems to be a hereditary trait in the family." It was noticeable in him: also in his brother Harrison-Gray[5] [see Nos. 148, 163,] and in the daughters of the latter. The residence of Hon. John Harris[5] was in Hopkinton village at the west end of Main street at the junction of the Henniker road. The house is somewhat elevated, and very conspicuous: it is now occupied by Reuben-E. French. "John Harris[†] owned the first floor carpet ever seen in Hopkinton. The introduction of this luxury ex-

---

* From J.-E. Pecker's letter to Boston *Journal*, May 8, 1876.

† Misses A.-B. and M.-B. Harris of Warner, N. H. have large oil portraits of Hon. John Harris[5] and his wife, painted probably seventy-five or more years ago. They have also the papers of Hon. John Harris[5].

cited unmeasured popular comment." He married, Sept., 1799, Mary Poor, daughter of Eliphalet and Elizabeth (Little) Poor, born in Hampstead, N. H., Feb. 10, 1779, died in Hopkinton, March 6, 1843.

CHILDREN, BORN IN HOPKINTON, N. H.

150.	George [171.], b. Feb. 6, 1801, d. Feb. 17, 1849, in Hopkinton, N. H.
151.	Catherine [172.], b. Jan. 23, 1804, d. Feb. 16, 1843, in Hopkinton, N. H.
152.	Eliza-Poor, b. Jan. 21, 1809, d. Oct. 31, 1850, in Concord, N. H.
153.	Anne, b. Feb. 19, 1812, d. Aug. 1, 1832, in Hopkinton, N. H.

154.	ASENATH[5] [143.] (Dea. Richard[4], Jr., Richard[3], Serjt. John[2], John[1]), married, June 19, 1796, CYRUS WHITNEY of Harvard, Mass. She died in Harvard, March 22, 1800. He married, 2, March 22, 1802, Polly Whitney of Harvard. Cyrus and Asenath (Harris[5]) Whitney had the following

CHILDREN, BORN IN HARVARD, MASS.

155.	Clarinda [175.], b. Oct. 24, 1797.
156.	Asena, b. March, 1800, d. Nov. 4, 1800.

157.	JOEL[5] [146.] (Dea. Richard[4], Jr., Richard[3], Serjt. John[2], John[1]), was born and died in Harvard, Mass. He graduated at Dartmouth College in 1804[*]; studied law with his brother, Hon. John Harris[5] [see Nos. 142, 149.], in Hopkinton, N. H.; began the practice of law there in 1807; removed to Harvard, Mass. in 1809, and practiced law there until his death. He lived in Harvard Center village, at the east corner of the Common. He married, Sept. 20, 1808, Mary Blood of Bolton, Mass. She was born in 1784, joined the Congregational church in Harvard, March 2, 1818, married, 2, Nov., 1847, Dea. James Kimball of Littleton, Mass., and died March 24, 1874.

CHILDREN.

158.	Mary, b. June 14, 1809, d. Nov. 20, 1817, in Harvard, Mass.
159.	Charlotte-Hayward [185.], b. Jan. 6, 1811, d. April 28, 1837, in New York, N. Y.

---

* He received the degree of Master of Arts in course, probably three years after graduation.

160. Horatio-Hayward, b. Dec. 3, 1812, d. March 29, 1833.
161. Frederic-William, b. Dec. 19, 1814, d. Feb. 12, 1817, in Harvard.
162. Anna-Maria, b. Feb. 20, 1817, d. Dec. 1, 1817, in Harvard; buried with her father.

163. HARRISON-GRAY⁶ [148.] (Dea. Richard⁵, Jr., Richard⁴, Serjt. John², John¹), was born in Harvard, Mass., and died in Warner, N. H. The following account of his life was prepared by his daughter Amanda-Bartlett⁷ [see Nos. 165, 188.] :—"Left an orphan on the death of his mother (at the age of eleven) he went to Hopkinton, N. H. to live with his brother John⁶ [see Nos. 142, 149.]. He pursued his studies in the office of his brother, and studied law there and with his other brother Joel⁶ [see Nos. 146, 157.] in Harvard, Mass. He was in the office of Estes Howe at Sutton, Mass. as student at law from April to Dec., 1811, and from that time till Sept., 1812 in that of B. Taft, Jr. of Uxbridge, Mass. In 1815 he was in the office of Mr. Towne at Amherst, N. H., and had charge of the business of Hon. Charles-H. Atherton while he was absent in Congress. He was admitted to the bar in 1815, in his examination proving himself to have been a far more thorough student than is often the case. He began practice in Sutton, N. H. in 1816, but after a few months went to Warner, N. H. (the same year) where he spent the remainder of his life. As a lawyer he was remarkable for his penetration and his power of analysis. He saw all the bearings of a case, and his judgment was as accurate as his perceptions were swift. He seldom erred in his opinion of character or in his conclusions, and his arguments were masterpieces of fine intuition and logic.

"Although his training was scholarly, he had great taste for agriculture, and was extremely fond of out-of-door life, preferring to walk rather than ride, and always so observing that nothing escaped his eye. In the latter years of his life he relinquished the practice of law, becoming interested in the care of a small farm he owned, and being very fond of gardening. It is characteristic of the man that in the last summer of his life, at the age of eighty-four, he set out cur-

rant cuttings in his garden, and was as much engaged as in
his prime to plant fruit trees for "somebody who may come
after." He had no ambition for a political career, never
sought office, nor made himself conspicuous, but in all matters relating to the advancement of his townspeople he was
one of the foremost, always interested in the public schools
and helping in every kindred interest. He had a remarkable
memory, and was a great reader of history. His nature was
social and generous, he was noted for his hospitality and affability, and was always the defender of the wronged and
needy, a friend of the children, incapable of a base act.

"He was a Free Mason from early manhood, and had a
long and honorable record in the fraternity, being connected
with it for nearly sixty years. He received the degree of
Master Mason in Blazing Star Lodge, Concord, in 1815;
was Master of St. Peter's Lodge, Bradford, in 1819, and of
Warner Lodge in 1824. He was Grand Lecturer of the
Grand Lodge in 1820, and District Deputy Grand Master in
1821 and 1822; received the Royal Arch Degree in Trinity
Chapter May 15, 1816; was High Priest in 1821 and 1824,
and was a member from 1816 till his death. He was Grand
Scribe of the Grand Chapter in 1821; was one of the founders of Mount Horeb Commandery at Hopkinton in 1826, and
was the last survivor of that band of Templars. At the formation of the Grand Encampment of Knights Templars in
1826 he was an officer, and was re-elected several years. The
Harris Lodge in Warner, constituted Sept. 3, 1875, was
named in honor of Harrison-Gray° and John-Atherton Har-
ris° [see Nos. 164, 187.]".

He married Mary Bartlett, only daughter of Richard* and
Mary (Currier) Bartlett of Warner, born March 15, 1800,
died Jan. 29, 1843, in Warner.

---

* Richard Bartlett was the leading magistrate of Warner. He served several years in the army of the Revolution; was liberal in works of charity.
His father was Simeon, a brother of Hon. Josiah Bartlett of Kingston, N. H.,
the second signer of the Declaration of Independence, and the first Governor

CHILDREN, BORN IN WARNER, N. H.

164.   John-Atherton [187.], b. Nov. 8, 1822, d. Sept. 3, 1877.
165.   Amanda-Bartlett [188.], b. Aug. 15, 1824.
166.   Augustus-Gray [189.], b. April 8, 1831.
167.   Franklin [193.], b. Sept. 20, 1833.
168.   Henry, b. Sept. 30, 1836, d. Sept. 21, 1837, in Warner.
169.   Mary-Bartlett [195.], b. June 20, 1838.
170.   Henry-Lawton [196.], b. Aug. 3, 1840.

SIXTH GENERATION.

171.   GEORGE⁶ [150.] (John⁵, Dea. Richard⁴, Jr., Richard⁴, Serjt. John², John¹), "lost his health early in life, by hard study, and became a life-long invalid. He was a very fine scholar, and was master of several languages. He fitted young men for college, and continued his habits of study, and kept pace with general literature all through his life. He was the second postmaster of Hopkinton, N. H., being appointed in place of his father, who resigned Aug. 4, 1824, and he held the office till July 6, 1829."

172.   CATHERINE⁶ [151.] (John⁵, Dea. Richard⁴, Jr., Richard⁴, Serjt. John², John¹), married, Dec. 6, 1832, Timothy-Wiggin Little, (a distant relative to her,) son of Maj. William and Eliza (Wiggin) Little, born Feb. 9, 1805, died April 12, 1863. He was a trader, settled in Hopkinton, N. H., where Catherine⁶ died. He married, 2, Mary-L. Britton, by whom he had two children; he removed to Manchester, N. H., before he died. Timothy-Wiggin and Catherine (Harris⁶) Little had the following

CHILDREN, BORN IN HOPKINTON, N. H.

173.   Mary-Poor, d. aged about 18 months.
174.   Elizabeth-Wiggin, b. 1834, d. July 6, 1854.

175.   CLARINDA WHITNEY⁶ [155.] (Asenath⁵ (Whitney), Dea. Richard⁴, Jr., Richard⁴, Serjt. John², John¹), married,

of New Hampshire, in 1792. Simeon was an ardent patriot, and chairman of the "Committee of Safety" during the long struggle for American independence. He was for many years one of the prominent business men of Amesbury, Mass., and was one of the original proprietors of the town of Warner, N. H., thereby owning one sixty-third part of the town.

Sept. 20, 1817, NATHAN WOODBURY of Bolton, Mass., son of Israel and Anna (Morgan) Woodbury; he was born in Bolton, Aug. 13, 1794, died in Rindge, N. H. Nov. 10, 1877. They removed in 1835 to a farm in the south part of Rindge, where Mrs. Woodbury still lives (March, 1883), aged over 85.

CHILDREN.

176. Asenath-Harris [198.]. b. April 17, 1819, in Harvard, Mass.
177. Mary-Ann [206.]. b. Jan. 16, 1821, in Pittston, Maine.
178. Nathan-Gray [208.]. b. April 16, 1823, in Pittston, Maine.
179. Harrison, b. March 19, 1826, in Bolton, Mass., d. Oct. 10, 1830.
180. Lauretta-Whitney [210.]. b. May 20, 1828, in Stow, Mass.
181. Lucinda-Bailey [212.]. b. Feb. 4, 1832, in Stow, Mass.
182. Clarinda-Augusta [215.]. b. March 23, 1834, in Lancaster, Mass.
183. Maria-Antonette [219.]. b. May 20, 1837, in Rindge, N. H.
184. Andrew-Cyrus, b. Dec. 25, 1840, in Rindge, N. H.; is a hotel-clerk; has been four winters employed in a hotel in Jacksonville, Fla., four summers in Cooperstown, N. Y., and one winter at Old Point Comfort, Va.

185. CHARLOTTE-HAYWARD[6] [159.] (Joel[5], Dea. Richard[4], Jr., Richard[3], Serjt. John[2], John[1]), married, May 5, 1836, WILLIAM-C. ALLEN, born in Townsend, Mass., in 1811, died in Pittsfield, Mass., Dec. 24, 1873. He was an importer of dry goods in New York city, and had a country seat at Pittsfield, Mass.; was a wealthy and prominent man.

CHILD, BORN IN NEW YORK, N. Y.

186. William-Horatio [222.]. b. April 21, 1837.

187. JOHN-ATHERTON[6] [164.] (Harrison-Gray[5], Dea. Richard[4], Jr., Richard[3], Serjt. John[2], John[1]). His sister Amanda-B. Harris[6] [see Nos. 165, 188.] writes of him:— "He received only an academic education and left school when quite young to become clerk in a country store; soon after, going to Boston, where he was engaged in the dry goods trade, as he was also in Waltham and Lowell, Mass. About 1850 he removed to Concord, N. H., where he went into business for himself, and where he resided during the remainder of his life, and died there. Though he had but

scant leisure from business duties he was a great reader of
the best authors and gradually gathered a choice library. His
tastes were those of a scholar: he was a careful critic, and in
the few reports and other papers of his which were printed,
the style is remarkable for its conciseness and vigor, and the
exact fitness of every word for its place. In the retentiveness
of his memory, his accuracy and keen logical powers and
thoroughness, he closely resembled his father, having inherited also in large measure charity towards his fellow-men,
generosity, affability, and unselfishness."

"He was one of the most distinguished Free Masons of
New England", as we learn from the Boston *Journal* of
Sept. 3, 1877, which also says:—"He was a member of va-
rious Masonic bodies, filled many official positions, and the
offices to which he had been called in the Grand bodies of
New Hampshire constitute one of the most honored records
that has ever fallen to a member of the fraternity in New
England*. As a Masonic historian he was without an equal
in his State. At the time of his death he was Secretary and
Recorder of five Grand bodies, a circumstance that has probably never before occurred in the Masonic history of his State.
In general historical matters he took a deep interest. He had
long been a member, and frequently held official positions in
the New Hampshire Historical Society, and his library was

---

* "In the Grand Lodge he was Lecturer in the Concord District from 1865
to 1869; R. W. Junior Grand Warden in 1870 and 1871; R. W. State Grand Lecturer in 1871; R. W. Senior Grand Warden in 1872, and since 1873 R. W.
Grand Secretary.—In the Grand Royal Arch Chapter he was R. A. Captain
in 1865, E. Grand Captain of the Host in 1866, E. Grand King in 1867 and
1868, E. Deputy Grand High Priest in 1869, M. E. Grand High Priest in 1870
and 1871, and from 1873, E. Grand Secretary.—In the Council of High Priests
of the State of New Hampshire he was Master of Ceremonies in 1869 and
1872, Vice President in 1870 and 1871, and Secretary since 1873.—In the Grand
Council of Royal and Select Masters he was Captain of the Guard in 1868,
Ill. Conductor in 1869, Ill. Grand Master in 1870, Deputy Puissant Grand
Master in 1871, Deputy Grand Master in 1872, M. P. Grand Master in 1873
and 1874, and Grand Recorder from 1875.—In the Grand Commandery he
had been E. Gr. Recorder since 1870. In the Scottish Masonry he had been
Ill. Grand Hospitaller of the Council of Deliberation".—Boston *Journal*,
Sept. 3, 1877.

very rich in ancient volumes kindred to such a sphere of thought and study."

188.   AMANDA-BARTLETT[6] [165.] (Harrison-Gray[5], Dea. Richard[4], Jr., Richard[3], Serjt. John[2], Thomas[1]), lives with her sister Mary-Bartlett[6] [see Nos. 169, 195.] on the "Harris Homestead" bought by their father in 1822, situated in Warner village, N. H. Her sister has furnished the following account of her life :—"She made her first venture in print over the signature of 'Venetia' in 1844 in the *New Hampshire Patriot*, then edited by Gov. Hill.   And from that time to the present, with long intervals (numbering years) of silence, she has contributed to many journals and periodicals, under different pseudonyms, rarely using her own name until 1874—the only material exception being in the case of a prize story, 'The Gypsy Queen,' published in *The American Union* (Boston) in 1849, when she took the second prize of $30, the first being awarded to C.-C. Hazewell, the third to J.-T. Trowbridge.   She has used at different times the pen-names, 'Ada Grey', 'Ina', 'Ina Bell', 'Kitty Carroll', and 'Kirkland'; and had many anonymous articles in Morris and Willis' *Home Journal* (New York), one of which, 'The Jewelled Hand', attracted considerable attention ; and her first contribution to the *Sabbath at Home* (Boston), 'The Female Friends of Our Saviour,' in 1867 was without name.   There is also a little book of hers published anonymously, 'The Duty of Uniting with the Church', which followed two under her own name, 'Christ Our Friend', and 'Thy Will be Done', all published by the American Tract Society (Boston).

"By the death of her mother she was left before the age of nineteen in charge of the family of four little children, and was the housekeeper for her father from then till his death. Many years ago her health broke down, and all her later, as well as earlier work has been done in odd hours under pressure of cares and many duties, and at extreme disadvantage. Under the circumstances the amount is surprising.   The subjects have been various, it has often been enforced labor, and the quality is by no means uniform. Besides occasional articles to other newspapers she has written for *The Christian Union*, *Illustrated Christian Weekly*, *Hearth and Home*, *Youth's Companion*, *Congregationalist*, and *New York Evening Post*, and since 1877 has been a constant reviewer of books for *The Literary World*. She has also had articles in several magazines, chief of which are *The Lady's Book*, *The Galaxy*, *Sabbath at Home*, *Appleton's Journal*, *Congregational Review*, *Good Company*, *St. Nicholas*, and *Wide Awake*. Solitary articles have been included in the contents of miscellaneous volumes: *The Opal* for 1848 (edited by Mrs. Sarah-J. Hale), 'Gems for You' (from New Hampshire authors), and several volumes published by D. Lothrop & Co. of Boston, Mass.

"In 1880, D. Lothrop & Co. published a handsome holiday volume by Miss Harris, beautifully illustrated by George-F. Barnes, entitled 'How We Went Birds'-nesting, or Field, Wood, and Meadow Rambles',—reprinted from *Wide Awake*. In 1881, at the request of the same publishers, she (with the aid of her sister) edited the 'Autograph Birthday Book for Young People', and 'Little Folks' Every Day Book'. In 1882, the same house published another holiday volume called 'Wild Flowers and Where They Grow'— also reprinted from *Wide Awake*—with illustrations by Miss L.-B. Humphrey, a part of them being local sketches of the scenes described. A new edition of the first named holiday book was issued at the same time, with the second title 'Field, Wood, and Meadow Rambles'. In 1883 D. Lothrop & Co. published a book for children by her, entitled 'Door Yard Folks'. The latest work upon which Miss Harris has been engaged is a series of twelve papers called 'Pleasant Authors for Young Folks'. June 9, 1880, she was made a member of the New Hampshire Historical Society, being the first woman ever admitted. July 19, 1881, she and her sister were elected members of the

New Hampshire Antiquarian Society". Rev. Edward-P. Tenney, D. D., President of Colorado College, mentions her in "Agamenticus" as "a literary friend of very rare skill with her pen." Her style of writing is peculiarly graceful and attractive. In religious views she adheres to the faith of her ancestors, being a member of the Congregational church.

189. AUGUSTUS-GRAY[6] [166.] (Harrison-Gray[5], Dea. Richard[4], Jr., Richard[3], Serjt. John[2], Thomas[1]), is a dealer in boots and shoes, and resides in Concord, N. H. He became clerk in a store in 1849, went to Concord in 1855, where he has since been in business. He has taken a great interest in Masonry, and held various offices in the order: is a Knight Templar. He married, Dec. 14, 1864, Sarah-Neal Jefts, daughter of George-W. and Minerva (Neal) Jefts, born in Hampton, N. H., May 4, 1841. Mrs. Harris is a teacher of elocution, oratory and dramatic art, giving lessons to private pupils.

CHILDREN, BORN IN CONCORD, N. H.

190.   Edward-Neal, b. Sept. 10, 1865, d. Sept. 10, 1867, in Hampton, N. H.
191.   Arthur-Henry, b. Dec. 5, 1868.
192.   Julia-Atherton, b. April 29, 1871.

193. FRANKLIN[6] [167.] (Harrison-Gray[5], Dea. Richard[4], Jr., Richard[3], Serjt. John[2], Thomas[1]), has lived in the West for many years, and at present resides in Minneapolis, Minn.; is a painter and paper-hanger. He married, Feb. 10, 1869, Mary-A. Coombs, daughter of William-Henry and Sarah (Evans) Coombs, born in New York, N. Y., Jan. 3, 1847.

CHILD, BORN IN NEW YORK, N. Y.

194.   William-Henry, b. Feb., 1870, d. Feb., 1870, in New York.

195. MARY-BARTLETT[6] [169.] (Harrison-Gray[5], Dea. Richard[4], Jr., Richard[3], Serjt. John[2], Thomas[1]), lives with her sister Amanda-Bartlett[6] [see Nos. 165, 188.] on the family homestead in Warner, N. H. The fine old mansion contains many things of historic and literary interest. In daily use in

their kitchen is the first stove that was brought into the town, bought in Feb., 1827. They own a large and very valuable library consisting of eleven hundred volumes, besides many pamphlets. Some of the books are of great value on account of their age and rarity*. Mary-Bartlett Harris⁶ taught school a few years in Warner, commencing at the age of sixteen. She aids her sister in literary work; was elected a member of the New Hampshire Antiquarian Society July 19, 1881. She owns a large and very valuable collection of autographs, numbering about five hundred specimens, especially rich in autograph letters of American and English authors, and of men prominent in New Hampshire half a century ago; it includes the autograph of every Governor of the state with one exception.

196. HENRY-LAWTON⁶ [170.] (Harrison-Gray⁵, Dea. Richard⁴, Jr., Richard³, Serjt. John², Thomas¹), was in the Civil war; enlisted in the 18th New Hampshire Regiment, commanded by Col. Clough, Sept. 23, 1864; mustered in Sept. 24; was promoted to Commissary Sergeant, Nov. 28, 1864; discharged June 10, 1865. He was appointed Brigade Commissary of the 1st Brigade Regiment of the New Hampshire National Guard, with the rank of Captain, Aug. 11, 1881, a position he still holds. He is a Knight Templar; has held offices in Masonic bodies. He has been in business for himself in Concord and Warner, N. H.; is at present employed in the wholesale shoe store of Batchelder & Lincoln in Boston, Mass. He married, Jan. 15, 1879, Caroline-Warren George, daughter of Charles and Margaret (Warren) George, born June 14, 1844.

CHILD, BORN IN BOSTON, MASS.

197. Katharine-Barnabee, b. Dec. 27, 1881.

---

*Among these are a copy of the Psalms, printed in 1635, "Burton's Anatomy of Melancholy", 1638, another rare book printed in 1657, and a copy of the first collected edition of Shakspeare's plays, printed in 1709.

SEVENTH GENERATION.

198. ASENATH-HARRIS WOODBURY[7] [176.] (Clarinda Whitney[6] (Woodbury), Asenath[5] (Whitney), Dea. Richard[4], Jr., Richard[3], Serjt. John[2], Thomas[1]), married, Nov. 28, 1839, ALBERT MANN, a farmer; they reside in Winchendon, Mass.

CHILDREN, BORN IN WINCHENDON, MASS.

199. Albert-Henry, born Feb. 8, 1841, d. April 6, 1842.
200. Julia-Lovejoy [226.], b. April 17, 1843.
201. Albert-Chester, b. March 2, 1845, d. July 17, 1845.
202. Oliver-Eugene, b. June 2, 1847, d. Sept. 2, 1847.
203. Albert-Eugene [227.], b. April 28, 1849.
204. Clara-Emma [228.], b. April 15, 1851, d. Sept. 24, 1873.
205. Oliver-Lovejoy, b. April 2, 1855; is a teamster; lives in Winchendon.

206. MARY-ANN WOODBURY[7] [177.] (Clarinda Whitney[6] (Woodbury), Asenath[5] (Whitney), Dea. Richard[4], Jr., Richard[3], Serjt. John[2], Thomas[1]), married, Sept. 19, 1842, SAMUEL PAGE, son of Levi Page. He is a carpenter and they live in Winchendon, Mass.

CHILD, BORN IN WINCHENDON, MASS.

207. George-Leslie, b. Jan. 7, 1855, d. Feb. 7, 1855.

208. NATHAN-GRAY WOODBURY[7] [178.] (Clarinda Whitney[6] (Woodbury), Asenath[5] (Whitney), Dea. Richard[4], Jr., Richard[3], Serjt. John[2], Thomas[1]), resides in Keene, N. H., and is a manufacturer of wooden pails, employing about seventy-five men in this industry; is also an undertaker, and is in company with another gentleman in the furniture business. He married, Dec. 31, 1849, Angelia Bryant of Richmond, N. H.

CHILD, BORN IN RICHMOND, N. H.

209. Edward-Calvin, b. Jan. 29, 1854, d. Jan. 24, 1865, in Richmond.

210. LAURETTA-WHITNEY WOODBURY[7] [180.] (Clarinda Whitney[6] (Woodbury), Asenath[5] (Whitney), Dea. Richard[4], Jr., Richard[3], Serjt. John[2], Thomas[1]), married, Dec. 28, 1852, NELSON PARKS of Winchendon, Mass., a machinist; they reside in Lynn, Mass.

CHILD, BORN IN WINCHENDON, MASS.

211. Flora-Josephine, b. Jan. 1, 1856, d. March 10, 1883, in Lynn, Mass.

212. LUCINDA-BAILEY WOODBURY[7] [181.] (Clarinda Whitney[6] (Woodbury), Asenath[5] (Whitney), Dea. Richard[4], Jr., Richard[3], Serjt. John[2], Thomas[1]), married, Dec. 30, 1863, HENRY-J. NEWMAN, a farmer; they removed in Aug., 1873, to her parents' homestead in Rindge, N. H., where they now reside.

CHILDREN, BORN IN WINCHENDON, MASS.

213. Hattie-Arvilla, b. Sept. 30, 1866,
214. Laforest-Nathan, b. Aug. 28, 1868.

215. CLARINDA-AUGUSTA WOODBURY[7] [182.] (Clarinda Whitney[6] (Woodbury), Asenath[5] (Whitney), Dea. Richard[4], Jr., Richard[3], Serjt. John[2], Thomas[1]), married, Oct. 7, 1858, DANIEL-H. SARGENT of Dunbarton, N. H., dealer in wood and lumber; they live in Rindge, N. H.

CHILDREN.

216. Edwin-Harris, b. Aug. 21, 1859, in Dunbarton, N. H.; is a carpenter in Rindge.
217. George-Arthur, b. June 16, 1862, in Dunbarton, N. H.; is a clerk in a jewelry store in Fitchburg, Mass.
218. Estella-Augusta, b. July 12, 1869, in Rindge, N. H.

219. MARIA-ANTENETTE WOODBURY[7] [183.] (Clarinda Whitney[6] (Woodbury), Asenath[5] (Whitney), Dea. Richard[4], Jr., Richard[3], Serjt. John[2], Thomas[1]), married, Nov. 21, 1859, GEORGE-F. WALLACE, provision dealer. He was the son of David Wallace; was born in Ashby, Mass., Nov. 21, 1833, died in Winchendon, Mass., July 10, 1874. His widow lives in Winchendon.

CHILDREN.

220. Hattie-Maria, b. Dec. 7, 1861, in Rindge, N. H., d. March 5, 1862, in Rindge.
221. Nellie-Etta, b. March 30, 1866, in Fitchburg, Mass.

222. WILLIAM-HORATIO ALLEN[7] [186.] (Charlotte-Hayward[6] (Allen), Joel[5], Dea. Richard[4], Jr., Richard[3], Serjt. John[2], Thomas[1]), is a hackman at the Rockingham House,

Portsmouth. N. H.   He married, Nov. 30, 1871, Eliza Jones, born in Newington, N. H., in 1845.

CHILDREN, BORN IN PORTSMOUTH, N. H.

223.   Fred-Jones, b. Nov. 9, 1873.
224.   Charles-Harris, b. Oct. 17, 1878.
225.   Emma-Belle, b. March 20, 1880.

EIGHTH GENERATION.

226.   JULIA-LOVEJOY MANN [200.] (Asenath-Harris Woodbury⁷ (Mann), Clarinda Whitney⁶ (Woodbury), Asenath⁵ (Whitney), Dea. Richard⁴, Jr., Richard³, Serjt. John², Thomas¹), married, Dec. 25, 1871, GEORGE KEMPTON ; they live in Lawrence, Mass.

227.   ALBERT-EUGENE MANN [203.] (Asenath-Harris Woodbury⁷ (Mann), Clarinda Whitney⁶ (Woodbury), Asenath⁵ (Whitney), Dea. Richard⁴, Jr., Richard³, Serjt. John², Thomas¹), lives in Winchendon, Mass. : is a teamster. He married, 1, Feb. 20, 1873, Mary Goodell of Orange, Mass. ; she died, Feb. 11, 1880. He married, 2, Sept. 28, 1881, Mabel-C. Foye of Andover, Maine.

CHILD, BORN IN WINCHENDON, MASS.

227½.   Mary-Isabella, b. Nov. 15, 1882.   She is in the *ninth generation* in America from Thomas Harris¹.   (See Nos. 618, 620.)

228.   CLARA-EMMA MANN [204.] (Asenath-Harris Woodbury⁷ (Mann), Clarinda Whitney⁶ (Woodbury), Asenath⁵ (Whitney), Dea. Richard⁴, Jr., Richard³, Serjt. John², Thomas¹), married, June 8, 1873, CHARLES BURGESS, and died in Sept. after.   He is a painter, and lives in Winchendon, Mass.

CHAPTER VIII.

FOURTH GENERATION.—REBECCA HARRIS (SCOLLAY).—
HER DESCENDANTS.

229. REBECCA HARRIS[4] [8.] (Richard[3], Serjt. John[2], Thomas[1]), was born in Harvard, Mass., March 25, 1748; baptized there March 27[*]; died in Rindge, N. H., March 21, 1819. She married, Nov. 4, 1779, GROVER SCOLLAY of Harvard. He was the second son of John Scollay,[†] who came from Scotland and settled in Stoneham, Mass. Grover was born Oct. 10, 1729, and died in Rindge, N. H., Jan. 19, 1816; he married, 1, Feb. 19, 1752, Lois Atherton, daughter of John and Phebe (Wright) Atherton of Harvard. Phebe married, 2, Richard Harris[3] [see No. 1.]. Lydia Atherton, sister to Lois, married Dea. Richard Harris[4], Jr. [see Nos. 6, 141.]. Grover and Lois Scollay joined the Congregational church in Harvard, probably in 1754; they had nine children.[‡] Lois died in Harvard, Sept. 7, 1778, and Grover married, 2, Rebecca Harris[4]. She joined the church

---

[*]Harvard First Church Records. Probably old style, or April 7 new style.
[†]John Scollay[1], the emigrant ancestor, had the following children :—
  1. John[2], died unmarried.
  2. Grover[2], b. Oct. 10, 1729, d. Jan. 19, 1816. [See No. 229.]
  3. Hannah[2], married John Shaw.
  4. Sarah[2], married Charles Willard.
  5. Anna[2], died unmarried.
[‡]The children of Grover[2] and Lois (Atherton) Scollay were as follows, all born in Harvard, Mass. :—
  1. John[3], b. Aug. 19, 1754, baptized Aug. 26, 1754.
  2. Ann[3], bapt. April 18, 1756.
  3. Sarah[3], bapt. March 4, 1759.

in Harvard Jan. 5, 1783. They removed from Harvard to Ashburnham, Mass., between March, 1783 and March, 1786, as their two older children were born in Harvard, and the three younger in Ashburnham.

CHILDREN.

230.   Samuel [235.], b. Jan. 21, 1781, d. Jan. 11, 1857.
231.   James [244.], b. March 24, 1783, d. Dec. 1, 1852.
232.   Ezra [251.], b. March 8, 1786, d. Nov. 10, 1874.
233.   Lucy [252.], b. March 31, 1788, d. Sept., 1842.
234.   Abel [255.], b. June 16, 1790, d. in Canada ?

FIFTH GENERATION.

1.   John , bapt. April 17, 1763; m. Esther Thwing, and had children :—1, Lucy-Hemenway; 2, Sarah-Chamberlin, who m. Elijah Clark, and now lives in Newton, Mass.; 3, John-George.
5.   Lois , bapt. Feb. 2, 1766.
6.   Lydia , bapt. Feb. 26, 1769.
7.   Betsey , bapt. Sept. 1, 1771.
8.   Lucy , bapt. Oct. 9, 1774.
9.   Grover , bapt. May 16, 1779; m., 1, Sally Dickinson, and had children : 1, Amos; 2, Sally; 3, Leonard; 4, Nancy; 5, Lucy. He m., 2, Sally Stowell, who now lives in Templeton, Mass.; their children were,—6, George; 7, Susan; 8, Clara; 9, Mary; 10, Milton; 11, Charles; 12, Albert; 13, Edwin; 14, Elmira; 15, Joseph; 16, Lucinda. Of these, Susan m. Dr. Edwin Leigh of Brooklyn, N. Y.

Sam'l Lee Clay

235. SAMUEL SCOLLAY[5] [230.] (Rebecca[4] (Scollay), Richard[3], Serjt. John[2], Thomas[1]), was born in Harvard, Mass., Jan. 21; baptized there July 1, 1781; a few years later his parents removed to Ashburnham, Mass.; he died in Smithfield, Virginia.   He graduated at Harvard College in 1808. His daughter, Mrs. Elizabeth Page[6] [see Nos. 240, 270.], writes of him:—"It seems he did not get a diploma at Harvard—though entitled to one—as it was necessary to pay quite a sum of money for them, and he could not spare the money. He had ambition and high aspirations which urged him on through many difficulties.   After he graduated at Harvard I suppose it was necessary for him to teach in order to make money to attend the medical lectures in Philadelphia.   So he taught in Harry Turner's family, five or six miles from Charlestown, Jefferson Co., Virginia, now West Virginia, and studied medicine under Dr. Samuel-J. Cramer of Charlestown.   I suppose he taught in this family two or three years, as it would take that length of time to prepare for the lectures in Philadelphia.

"He graduated in medicine at the University of Pennsylvania, in Philadelphia, in the spring of 1816.   When he graduated he located in Smithfield, Jefferson Co., Virginia, and practiced medicine.   Afterwards his son Charles-Lowndes[7] [see Nos. 236, 258.] practiced with him.   He always cherished a warm affection for, and interest in, his *alma mater*.   He was one of the most distinguished physicians in Jefferson County, and died worth one hundred thousand dollars; he continued the practice of medicine in Smithfield until the fall before his death.   His descendants are all, in religious preference, adherents of the Protestant Episcopal Church." The original of the accompanying portrait of Dr. Samuel Scollay was taken in 1850, when he was nearly seventy years of age. The silhouette, of which a copy is shown on the preceding page, was cut in 1822.   His autograph, of which a fac-simile is presented, was written in 1856.

He married, 1, Jan. 21, 1822, Harriot Lowndes, daughter of Charles* and Eleanor (Lloyd†) Lowndes, born in Georgetown, D. C., Nov. 23, 1794, and died in Smithfield, Va., August 5, 1835.

CHILDREN, BORN IN SMITHFIELD, VA.

236. Charles-Lowndes [258.], b. Oct. 1, 1823, d. July 12, 1857, in Smithfield.
237. Anne-Lloyd [259.], b. Aug. 13, 1825, d. April 3, 1868, in Charlestown, W. Va.
238. Samuel-Storrow, b. March 3, 1827, d. Oct. 10, 1831, in Smithfield.
239. Eleanor-Grover [266.], b. July 22, 1829, d. Oct. 9, 1855, in Summit Point, Va.
240. Elizabeth [270.], b. June 21, 1831.

He married, 2, Jan. 21, 1841, Sally-Page Nelson, a granddaughter of Gen. Thomas Nelson‡ of Yorktown, Va., one of the signers of the Declaration of Independence from Virginia, a general in the Revolutionary Army [see Nos. 270, 281, foot-notes.]. She was born in Hanover Co., Va., Dec. 10, 1801, and now (March, 1883) lives in Smithfield, W. Va.

CHILDREN, BORN IN SMITHFIELD, VA.

241. Francis-Nelson, b. Nov. 24, 1841, d. Aug. 1, 1845, in Smithfield.
242. Harriot-Lowndes [273.], b. May 11, 1843.
243. Mary-Nelson [281.], b. Oct. 15, 1844.

244. JAMES SCOLLAY' [231.] (Rebecca⁴ (Scollay), Richard³, Serjt. John², Thomas¹), was born in Harvard, Mass., March 24; baptized there March 30, 1783. His parents removed to Ashburnham, Mass., when he was an infant. He was a farmer, and went from Ashburnham and settled in the east part of Gardner, Mass. He married, April 2, 1807, Dolly Corey.

CHILDREN, BORN IN GARDNER, MASS.

245. Dolly [291.], b. Nov. 8, 1808, d. Oct. 25, 1843.

*Charles Lowndes was a grandson of John Lowndes, Gent. of "Bostock House", Cheshire, England. Charles Lowndes' son Lloyd Lowndes of Clarksburg, W. Va., was the father of Hon. Lloyd Lowndes of Cumberland, Md., a member of the 43rd Congress.

†Eleanor Lloyd was the daughter of Gov. Edward Lloyd of Maryland. Eleanor's sister, Mary Lloyd, married Francis-Scott Key, who was the author of "The Star-Spangled Banner."

‡See Appleton's American Cyclopedia.

246.   Sarah [294.], b. Sept. 10, 1810, d. Jan. 26, 1870.
247.   James [296.], b. March 26, 1812, d. Jan. 14, 1874.
248.   Charles [301.], b. Jan. 8, 1814.
249.   Lucy [302.], b. Aug. 26, 1816, d. Nov. 19, 1846.
250.   Ezra, b. April 9, 1821, d. Nov. 26, 1841.

251.   EZRA SCOLLAY[5] [232.] (Rebecca[4] (Scollay), Richard[3], Serjt. John[2], Thomas[1]), was born in Ashburnham, Mass., lived in Rindge, N. H. most of his life, and died in New Ipswich, N. H.   He married, 1, Dec. 31, 1807, Mersilva Jewett, the second daughter of Dea. Edward Jewett, a prominent man of Rindge.   She was born Nov. 4, 1786, and died June 2, 1855 ; was "a lady of most excellent character and intellectual gifts."   He married, 2, Oct. 14, 1856, Polly Hale, daughter of David and Bathsheba (Barker) Hale, who was born Feb. 8, 1788, and died Dec. 17, 1866.   He married, 3, Sept. 19, 1867, Mrs. Mary-P. Moore of New Ipswich, N. H., in which town he resided from the time of his third marriage until his death.

252.   LUCY SCOLLAY[5] [233.] (Rebecca[4] (Scollay), Richard[3], Serjt. John[2], Thomas[1]), was born in Ashburnham, and died in Leominster, Mass.   She married, March 24, 1823, ASA FARNSWORTH, a farmer ; lived in Leominster, where he died, June 18, 1831, aged 53.

CHILDREN, BORN IN LEOMINSTER, MASS.

253.   Dorothy [306.], b. March 17, 1826.
254.   Ezra-Scollay [308.], b. March 28, 1830.

255.   ABEL SCOLLAY[5] [234.] (Rebecca[4] (Scollay), Richard[3], Serjt. John[2], Thomas[1]), was born in Ashburnham, Mass. "He went away when young, and lived in Canada."   This is all that has been learned concerning his history except that in a family record kept by his brother Ezra[5], the record occurs of two of his

CHILDREN.

256.   Ezra, b. June 19, 1831, d. June 13, 1834.
257.   Mersilva-Jewett, b. Dec. 5, 1835, d. Dec. 1, 1841.

SIXTH GENERATION.

258. CHARLES-LOWNDES SCOLLAY⁶ [236.] (Dr. Samuel Scollay⁵, Rebecca⁴ (Scollay), Richard³, Serjt. John², Thomas¹), received his early education under family tutors, who were college graduates (of either Harvard or Princeton College). About two years before entering college he attended the Academy in Charlestown, Jefferson Co., Va. He graduated at Princeton College in 1845. He then studied medicine with his father, Samuel Scollay⁵, M. D. [see No. 235.], at Smithfield, Va., and graduated in medicine at the University of Pennsylvania in Philadelphia in 1848. He then engaged in the practice of medicine in company with his father in Smithfield, where he died before the age of 34.

259. ANNE-LLOYD SCOLLAY⁶ [237.] (Dr. Samuel Scollay⁵, Rebecca⁴ (Scollay), Richard³, Serjt. John², Thomas¹), married, June 21, 1843, GEORGE-HITE-JENNINGS BECKWITH; he is a farmer, and lives at "Shady Side" farm in Charlestown, Jefferson County, W. Va.

CHILDREN, BORN IN SMITHFIELD, VA.

260. Harriot-Lowndes, b. June 13, 1845, d. Sept. 29, 1847.
261. Samuel-Scollay, b. Nov. 30, 1846, d. April 29, 1873.
262. James-Francis [310.], b. July 26, 1848.
263. Sally-Madison [311.], b. Oct. 21, 1850.
264. Lawrence-Butler, b. Jan. 26, 1853; is a cotton-planter in Desha Co., Arkansas.
265. Eloise-Lowndes, b. March 13, 1855, d. July 9, 1878.
265½. Mary-Elizabeth, b. June 1, 1857; lives with her father at "Shady Side."

266. ELEANOR-GROVER SCOLLAY⁶ [239.] (Dr. Samuel Scollay⁵, Rebecca⁴ (Scollay), Richard³, Serjt. John², Thomas¹), married, Dec. 12, 1850, SAMUEL-JOHNSTON-CRAMER MOORE*, a lawyer, now practicing his profession in Berryville, Clarke Co., Va. "At fifteen years of age he entered a Clerk's office as Deputy Clerk, remaining until he was about twenty-two.

---

*He is a grandson of Dr. Samuel-Johnston Cramer of Charlestown, Va., with whom Dr. Samuel Scollay studied medicine [see No. 235.].

discharging the duties of his position, and devoting the hours of the early morning and of the night to study. At the age of twenty-one he obtained a license to practice law, and has mainly devoted his life to his profession since that time."

CHILDREN.

267. Eleanor-Cramer, b. Oct. 26, 1851, in Smithfield, Va., d. Sept. 6, 1852.
268. Samuel-Scollay [313,], b. Sept. 27, 1853, in Smithfield, Va.
269. Ellen-Scollay, b. Aug. 14, 1855, in Summit Point, Va., d. Oct. 25, 1856.

270. ELIZABETH SCOLLAY⁶ [240.] (Dr. Samuel Scollay⁵, Rebecca⁴ (Scollay), Richard³, Serjt. John², Thomas¹), married, Nov. 11, 1856, POWHATAN-ROBERTSON PAGE*, son of Mann and Judith-Page (Nelson†) Page, born in Gloucester Co., Va., June 29, 1821. He was a farmer, but had considerable military experience. When quite young he was in the Mexican war as First Lieutenant. He was Captain of a Volunteer Company in Gloucester Co., Va., and was ordered to Harper's Ferry by the Governor at the time of the John Brown raid. When Virginia seceded from the Union he was made Colonel of the 26th Regiment Virginia Volunteers, and was killed in battle at Petersburg, Va., June 17, 1864. His widow and daughter now live in Clarksburg, Harrison Co., W. Va.

CHILDREN, BORN AT "THE SHIPYARD", IN GLOUCESTER CO., VA.

271. Sally-Scollay, b. May 8, 1858.
272. Mann, b. Oct. 20, 1859, d. Nov. 7, 1859.

273. HARRIOT-LOWNDES SCOLLAY⁶ [242.] (Dr. Samuel Scollay⁵, Rebecca⁴ (Scollay), Richard³, Serjt. John², Thomas¹), married, Nov. 27, 1867, ALEXANDER-MASON EVANS, M. D. He graduated from the University of Pennsylvania in Philadelphia in March, 1876, and now practices medicine

*He was a great-grandson of Gov. John Page of "Rosewell" on York river in Gloucester Co., Va., who was "a distinguished statesman."

†Judith-Page Nelson was a cousin to her husband Mann Page before marriage. She was a grand-daughter of Gen. Thomas Nelson, signer of the Declaration of Independence; and was a sister to Sally-Page Nelson, who married Dr. Samuel Scollay [see No. 235.], and a cousin to Rev. G. W. Nelson, Sr [see No. 281, foot-note.].

in the town of Middleway or Smithfield, Jefferson Co., W. Va.

274. Mann-Nelson, b. March 29, 1869, d. July 14, 1869.
275. Mary-Mason, b. June 1, 1870.
276. Sally-Scollay, b. Oct. 18, 1872.
277. Lizzie-Page, b. Oct. 4, 1874.
278. Samuel-Scollay, b. Nov. 27, 1876, d. June 18, 1877.
279. Eleanor-Grover, b. April 3, 1878.
280. Harriot, b. Nov. 4, 1880.
280½. Margaret-Howell, b. Feb. 28, 1883.

281. MARY-NELSON SCOLLAY⁶ [243.] (Dr. Samuel Scollay⁵, Rebecca⁴ (Scollay), Richard³, Serjt. John², Thomas¹), married, Oct. 17, 1865, Rev. GEORGE-WASHINGTON NELSON, Jr.* He graduated at the School of Latin of the University of Virginia, in Albemarle County, in 1860, at the age of 20. He served as Captain of Artillery in General Lee's army during the Civil war; was engaged in farming and in teaching for several years. He graduated at the Theological Seminary of Virginia at Alexandria in June, 1874, and was ordained to the diaconate of the Protestant Episcopal Church the same month, and took charge of a parish the succeeding fall. He is now rector of the Episcopal church in Warrenton, Fauquier Co., Va.

CHILDREN.

282. Sally-Page, b. July 4, 1866.
283. Thomas-Crease, b. Jan. 7, 1868.
284. Harry-Lee, b. Oct. 5, 1869.
285. Charlotte-Cazenove, b. Sept. 16, 1871.
286. Jane-Crease, b. Dec. 15, 1873, d. Dec. 19, 1873.
287. George-Washington, b. July 29, 1875.
288. Philip, b. Sept. 21, 1878.
289. Samuel-Scollay, b. July 20, 1880.
290. Caroline-Peyton, b. May 26, 1882.

*His father, Rev. George-Washington Nelson, Sr. (an Episcopal minister), was a grandson of Gen. Thomas Nelson, signer of the Declaration of Independence, and was a cousin to Sally-Page Nelson, who married Dr. Samuel Scollay⁵ [see No. 235,], and also a cousin to Judith-Page Nelson [see No. 270.].

291.   DOLLY SCOLLAY[6] [245.] (James Scollay[5], Rebecca[4] (Scollay), Richard[3], Serjt. John[2], Thomas[1]), married, April 16, 1829, AMASA WHITNEY, son of William and Anna (Heywood) Whitney, born in Gardner, Mass., June 19, 1805, and died Jan. 21, 1871.   He was a farmer in Gardner, but had sufficient means to live without daily labor.

CHILDREN, BORN IN GARDNER, MASS.

292.   Charles [315.], b. Sept. 21, 1830.
293.   James, b. Oct. 4, 1835, d. Feb. 16, 1844, in Gardner.

294.   SARAH SCOLLAY[6] [246.] (James Scollay[5], Rebecca[4] (Scollay), Richard[3], Serjt. John[2], Thomas[1]), married, Nov. 21, 1810, DAVID PARKER, M. D., who was born March 18, 1802, and has practiced medicine in Gardner, Mass. since Oct., 1823, and is practicing there still.

CHILD, BORN IN GARDNER, MASS.

295.   Eliza [317.], b. Nov. 29, 1845.

296.   JAMES SCOLLAY[6], JUNIOR [247.] (James Scollay[5], Rebecca[4] (Scollay), Richard[3], Serjt. John[2], Thomas[1]), was a painter, and removed in 1839 to St. Louis, Mo., where he died in 1874.   He married, June 26, 1836, Lucy-Maria Young, daughter of Asa and Lucy-Maria Young, born in Portsmouth, N. H., Nov. 20, 1816: she still lives in St. Louis.

CHILDREN, BORN IN ST. LOUIS, MO.

297.   Lucy-Maria [319.], b. April 15, 1847.
298.   Emma-Blanche [320.], b. April 16, 1850.
299.   James [325.], b. Oct. 6, 1851.
300.   Charles [327.], b. Feb. 17, 1858.

301.   CHARLES SCOLLAY[6] [248.] (James Scollay[5], Rebecca[4] (Scollay), Richard[3], Serjt. John[2], Thomas[1]), is a chair-maker and lives in Gardner, Mass.   He married, Oct. 10, 1843, Elizabeth-A. Garfield, daughter of Enoch and Lucy (Hodgkings) Garfield, born in Troy, N. H., Dec. 27, 1816. (See No. 319.)

302.   LUCY SCOLLAY[6] [249.] (James Scollay[5], Rebecca[4] (Scollay), Richard[3], Serjt. John[2], Thomas[1]), married, Nov. 24, 1836, ALFRED-H. BRICK, a chair-dealer, and lived in Fitchburg, Mass.   He is the son of Elijah and Sally (Comer) Brick.

CHILDREN.

303.   Francis [329.], b. March 16, 1838, in Gardner, Mass.
304.   Eliza, b. Sept. 9, 1840, in Gardner, Mass., d. Dec. 8, 1840.
305.   Harriet-Shattuck [331.], b. Oct. 23, 1843, in New Ipswich, N. H.

306.   DOROTHY FARNSWORTH[6] [253.] (Lucy Scollay[5] (Farnsworth), Rebecca[4] (Scollay), Richard[3], Serjt. John[2], Thomas[1]), married, April 26, 1848, ABEL-C. CHASE, son of George and Sophronia Chase, born in Leominster, Mass., Feb. 1, 1824.   They live in Leominster.

CHILD, BORN IN LEOMINSTER, MASS.

307.   George-Metaphor, b. Nov. 27, 1850, d. Oct. 11, 1869, in Leominster.

308.   EZRA-SCOLLAY FARNSWORTH[6] [254.] (Lucy Scollay[5] (Farnsworth), Rebecca[4] (Scollay), Richard[3], Serjt. John[2], Thomas[1]), was born in Leominster, Mass., March 28, 1830, and now lives in Newton, Mass., doing business there and in Boston.   When young he lived in several places in Massachusetts.   In Dec., 1851 he went to New Orleans, La., remaining until May, 1852, when he went up the Mississippi river to Cincinnati, O., and remained during the summer, then returned to Watertown, Mass.; in 1854 he went into business in Newton, Mass.; four years later he went into business in Boston, still living in Newton.

"In July, 1862, he enlisted in the army as a private in a volunteer Company of which he was the instigator and on whose roll his was the first name.   The Company was assigned to the 32nd Regiment, Massachusetts Infantry.   In August he was appointed First Serjeant; was made Second Lieutenant March 19, 1863, First Lieutenant June 15, 1864, Captain July 20, 1864, and was brevetted Major by the President March 13, 1865; was discharged at the expiration of the three years' term of service, May 29, 1865. During his service in the army he was twice appointed Judge Advocate of Courts Martial; served several months as Adjutant of his regiment; was recruiting officer of the regiment when it re-enlisted for volunteers of the war; and the last six months was Acting Assistant Adjutant General of the 3rd Brigade 1st Division 5th Army Corps, the largest brigade in the army, and the brigade that had the honor of receiving the surrender of the Army of Northern Virginia at Appomattox Court House, Va., commanded by Gen. Lee. He was several times wounded, twice severely, once at Gettysburg, Va., and once at Laurel Hill, near Spotsylvania Court House, Va.

"After he came home to Newton in 1865 he went to St. Louis, Mo., where he remained nearly two years, being manager of the *St. Louis Dispatch*, a daily evening paper. He spent the summer of 1867 in Minnesota and Wisconsin; returned to Newton in Nov.; in Dec., 1867 went into the wholesale paper business, and remained three years; then engaged in his former business of real estate, in which he has since continued. He is real estate and insurance agent, auctioneer and appraiser; has been a Justice of the Peace and a Notary Public for Middlesex Co., Mass. since 1871." He married, May 22, 1854, Mary-Frances Brown, daughter of William and Mary Brown of Boston, Mass., born in Boston, Oct. 11, 1832.

CHILD, BORN IN NEWTON, MASS.

309. Mersylva-Ella, b. June 1, 1855, d. July 17, 1856, in Newton.

SEVENTH GENERATION.

310. JAMES-FRANCIS BECKWITH[7] [262.] (Anne-Lloyd Scollay[6] (Beckwith), Dr. Samuel Scollay[5], Rebecca[4] (Scollay), Richard[3], Serjt. John[2], Thomas[1]), is a lawyer, practicing his profession in Charlestown, Jefferson Co., W. Va. He attended in 1867 and 1868 the "Seminary of Our Lady of

Angels", a Catholic college at Niagara Falls, N. Y.; was admitted to the bar in 1872, in Charlestown. He was elected to the Legislature of West Virginia in the fall of 1880 for a term of two years, 1881-2, representing Jefferson County.

311. SALLY-MADISON BECKWITH⁷ [263.] (Anne-Lloyd Scollay⁶ (Beckwith), Dr. Samuel Scollay⁵, Rebecca⁴ (Scollay), Richard³, Serjt. John², Thomas¹), married, Jan. 6, 1881, TILDEN-GARNET BAYLOR. He entered the Virginia Military Institute at Lexington, Rockbridge Co., Va., in the fall of 1868 and graduated in the summer of 1871; is a civil engineer, employed at present on the Pittsburgh Southern Railroad in Pennsylvania.

CHILD, BORN IN CHARLESTOWN, W. VA.

312. Annie-Lloyd, b. Feb. 22, 1882.

313. SAMUEL-SCOLLAY MOORE⁷ [268.] (Eleanor-Grover Scollay⁶ (Moore), Dr. Samuel Scollay⁵, Rebecca⁴ (Scollay), Richard³, Serjt. John², Thomas¹). "was a student at the University of Virginia at Charlottesville during the session of 1872-3. In the fall of 1873 he commenced the study of law in the office of his father, Samuel-J.-C. Moore [see No. 266.], at Berryville, Va., and was admitted to the bar, after a year's study, in the fall of 1874. After obtaining a license to practice law, he went to Europe and spent a year in travel in Great Britain and on the Continent. On his return in Sept., 1875, he commenced the practice of law in Berryville, Va., in partnership with his father, and continued for several years. He held for a time, the office of Commissioner in Chancery, by appointment of the Court; and was elected Mayor of Berryville by the people for a term ending Jan. 1, 1880, he declining a re-election." After his wife's death in 1881, he gave up the practice of law, and in Sept., 1882, entered the Protestant Episcopal Theological Seminary at Alexandria, Va., intending to fit himself for the ministry of that

Church. He married, April 29, 1880, Elvira-J. McCormick, who died June 18, 1881.

CHILD, BORN IN BERRYVILLE, VA.

344. Edward, b. April 12, 1881.

315. CHARLES WHITNEY' [292.] (Dolly Scollay' (Whitney), James-Scollay', Rebecca' (Scollay), Richard', Serjt. John', Thomas'), resides on a farm in Gardner, Mass. He married, Dec. 2, 1857, Mary Knowlton, daughter of Emory and Polly (Fisher) Knowlton, born in Gardner, May 19, 1836.

CHILD, BORN IN GARDNER, MASS.

316. Charles-Emory, b. March 8, 1867.

317. ELIZA PARKER' [295.] (Sarah Scollay' (Parker), James Scollay', Rebecca' (Scollay), Richard', Serjt. John', Thomas'), married, June 3, 1873, FRANK-W. SMITH, a silversmith: they live in Concord, N. H.

CHILD, BORN IN CONCORD, N. H.

318. William-David, b. Dec. 18, 1876.

319. LUCY-MARIA SCOLLAY' [297.] (James Scollay', Jr., James Scollay', Rebecca' (Scollay), Richard', Serjt. John', Thomas'), lived from the age of fifteen months until her marriage, with her uncle, Charles Scollay' [see No. 304.], in Gardner, Mass. She married, Nov. 8, 1871, CHARLES-EDWIN GLAZIER, son of Thomas-Edwin and Lucy (Brown) Glazier, born in Gardner, Mass., June 6, 1839. He is a dealer in lumber, and they live in Athol, Mass.

320. EMMA-BLANCHE SCOLLAY' [298.] (James Scollay', Jr., James Scollay', Rebecca' (Scollay), Richard', Serjt. John', Thomas'), married, Nov. 29, 1868, CHARLES-WILLIAM BEEHLER, a machinist, and they live in St. Louis, Mo.

CHILDREN, BORN IN ST. LOUIS, MO.

321. John-Charles, b. Dec. 9, 1869.
322. Mary-Blanche, b. Aug. 3, 1871.

323. James-Francis, b. May 11, 1873.
324. Joseph-Edward, b. March 15, 1878, d. Aug. 16, 1882.

325. JAMES SCOLLAY[7], JUNIOR [299.] (James Scollay[6], Jr., James Scollay[5], Rebecca[4] (Scollay), Richard[3], Serjt. John[2], Thomas[1]), is a painter and lives in St. Louis, Mo. He married, Nov. 8, 1879, Margaret-V. Scott.

CHILD, BORN IN ST. LOUIS, MO.

326. Mabel, b. Aug. 17, 1880.

327. CHARLES SCOLLAY[7] [300.] (James Scollay[6], Jr., James Scollay[5], Rebecca[4] (Scollay), Richard[3], Serjt. John[2], Thomas[1]), is a machinist, and lives in St. Louis, Mo. He married, Dec. 28, 1880, Mary-Hunter Herries.

CHILD, BORN IN ST. LOUIS, MO.

328. Aimee, b. April 11, 1882.

329. FRANCIS BRICK[7] [303.] (Lucy Scollay[6] (Brick), James Scollay[5], Rebecca[4] (Scollay), Richard[3], Serjt. John[2], Thomas[1]), is a physician, practicing in Worcester, Mass. "He commenced the study of medicine with Dr. E.-J. Sawyer of Gardner, Mass., early in 1859; afterwards continued his studies with Dr. J.-C. Freeland of Fitchburg, Mass.; attended two courses of lectures at the Western Homeopathic College in Cleveland, O., graduating in Feb., 1861. In the spring of 1862 he commenced practice in Winchester, N. H., and in the summer of 1864 removed to Keene, N. H., remaining there, with the exception of a few months, until Jan., 1875, when he went to Worcester. He is a member of the American Institute of Homeopathy, the Worcester County Homeopathic Society, and the Massachusetts Surgical and Gynecological Society." He married, June 5, 1862, Helen-Frances Guild, born in Attleborough, Mass., May 16, 1843.

CHILD, BORN IN KEENE, N. H.

330. Lu-Guild, b. Feb. 29, 1872.

331. HARRIET-SHATTUCK BRICK[7] [305.] (Lucy Scollay[6] (Brick), James Scollay[5], Rebecca[4] (Scollay), Richard[3], Serjt. John[2], Thomas[1]), married, Nov. 29, 1865, CHARLES-A. WILSON, M. D., son of Wheaton and Jerusha Wilson, born in South Royalston, Mass., April 20, 1841. He received his early education in South Gardner, Mass., and graduated at Harvard Medical School in March, 1869. He commenced practice in West Cummington, Mass.; is now a practicing physician in Rome City, Noble Co., Indiana, and is also manager of Spring Beach Hotel and Sanitarium at that place.

CHILD, BORN IN WEST CUMMINGTON, MASS.

332. Charles-Frederick, b. Nov. 17, 1867.

CHAPTER IX.

FOURTH GENERATION.—NATHANIEL HARRIS.—HIS DESCEND-
ANTS.

333.   NATHANIEL HARRIS[4] [10.] (Richard[3], Serjt. John[2], Thomas[1]), was born in Harvard, Mass., April 4, 1752; baptized there April 5.   He settled in Ashburnham, Mass. when a young man,—as early as 1777, as he was "of Ashburnham" Nov. 2 of that year, when his intention of marriage was published.   His brother Jacob[1] [see Nos. 5, 17.] had settled in the same town some years before, and their sister Rebecca (Harris[4]) Scollay [see Nos. 8, 229.] afterwards removed there.   Nathaniel[1] lived in Ashburnham Center village on Main street.   The square, two-story house in which he (no doubt) lived, is still standing, and is owned and occupied by Nahum Woods.   His occupation while he remained in Ashburnham was that of a tanner; his tannery is supposed to have been in the village.   Dec. 13, 1797, he deeded to Abraham Lowe, M. D., pew No. 35 in the "public meetinghouse", in consideration of forty dollars.   The deed was acknowledged before a Justice, Jan. 9, 1798.   Between this date and Dec. 23, 1800, when his youngest child was born, he removed from Ashburnham to Brandon, Vermont, where he lived during the remainder of his life, and died there June 21, 1831, aged over 79, and having survived his wife and all his children.

*Harvard First Church Records.   Probably old style, or April 16, new style.

His home in Brandon was on a farm one mile north of the village—a very pleasant location. The house was burned a few years ago, and has not been rebuilt. His occupation there was farming. He joined the Congregational church in Ashburnham in 1782; March 3, 1811, was received into the Congregational church in Brandon, by letter from the former church. He is remembered as "an exemplary member of the church" in Brandon.* He married, March 12, 1778, Abigail Harris of Ashburnham, who, although of the same name, was not known to be related. She was born in Shrewsbury, Mass., July 1, 1756, and died in Brandon, Vt., March 5, 1826. Of their nine children, all were born in Ashburnham, Mass., except the youngest one, and all died in Brandon except the two oldest. Four of them died of canker-rash in May, 1805.

CHILDREN.

334. Nathaniel [343.], b. Dec. 29, 1778, d. Nov. 6, 1830.
335. Rufus [345.], b. Sept. 27, 1781, d. March 30, 1827.
336. Richard [350.], b. Nov. 8, 1783, d. Aug. 22, 1821.
337. Otis, b. Jan. 22, 1786, d. May 21, 1805.
338. Nabby, b. June 13, 1788, d. May 4, 1805.
339. Lucinda, b. Sept. 23, 1791, d. May 9, 1805.
340. Matilda, b. Feb. 8, 1795, d. May 2, 1805.
341. Rebecca, b. Sept. 7, 1797, d. July 17, 1803.
342. Sarah-Brigham, b. Dec. 23, 1800, in Brandon, d. July 12, 1805.

FIFTH GENERATION.

343. NATHANIEL[5], JUNIOR [334.] (Nathaniel[4], Richard[3], Serjt. John[2], Thomas[1]), was born in Ashburnham, Mass.; lived in Williston, Vt., where he kept a country store. He is also said to have been a shoe-maker, and a member of the Masonic fraternity. He was a member of the Congregational church in Williston; died in that town. He married, May 16, 1802, Sally Ives, who died in Williston, Jan. 13, 1826.

*His old family Bible—printed in 1793 by Isaiah Thomas—containing records of births and deaths, is now in the possession of his grand-daughter, Mrs. Lydia-G. Case, of Brandon, Vt. [See Nos. 355, 389.]

CHILD, BORN IN WILLISTON, VT.

344.   Cynthia-Lucinda [356.], b. Sept. 9, 1806, d. Feb. 19, 1845.

345.   RUFUS⁵ [335.] (Nathaniel⁴, Richard³, Serjt. John², Thomas¹), was born in Ashburnham, Mass.; died in Bridport, Vt. In early life he settled in Bridport, where he kept a country store, also owning a farm, and was for several years postmaster; was a member of the Congregational church in Bridport. He married, April 7, 1807, Mary Clayes, "a very superior lady, fully appreciating intellectual culture, and withal a lovely Christian character." She was the daughter of Peter* and Mary (Nixon) Clayes of Framingham, Mass., born in Framingham, July 20, 1785, and died in Bridport, Sept. 8, 1849, "much regretted by the entire community."

CHILDREN, BORN IN BRIDPORT, VT.

346.   Julius-Otis [360.], b. May 1, 1808, d. Dec. 23, 1869.
347.   Charles-Edwin [366.], b. Oct. 1, 1810.
348.   Emily-Sophia, b. Feb. 17, 1813, d. July 20, 1828, in Bridport.
349.   Mary-Nixon [368.], b. Sept. 26, 1817.

350.   RICHARD⁵ [356.] (Nathaniel⁴, Richard³, Serjt. John², Thomas¹), was born in Ashburnham, Mass., and died in Brandon, Vt. He strained his chest in chopping just before his marriage and was never well afterward. Finding after marriage that he was not able to carry on his father's farm as he had intended, he started a small store in Brandon, first having spent a short time in Bridport with his brother Rufus⁵ [see Nos. 335, 345.] in learning the business. He married, June 28, 1807, Hannah-Howe Goodnow. She was born Feb. 22, 1792, in Rutland, Mass., and went to Brandon from that town at the age of eleven with her father, Daniel Goodnow and his family. She died in Brandon, Dec. 12, 1867.

*Peter Clayes was a Captain in the army from the commencement to the close of the Revolutionary war. He died in Bridport, Vt. in the summer of 1834, aged 84.

351. Hannah-Almira [372.], b. Jan. 19, 1809, d. March 11, 1853.
352. Betsey-Matilda [378.], b. April 22, 1811, d. June 12, 1878.
353. Sarah-Louisa [381.], b. Sept. 25, 1814.
354. Richard-Appleton, b. June 23, 1819, d. July 28, 1834.
355. Lydia-Goodnow [389.], b. Oct. 10, 1820.

SIXTH GENERATION.

356. CYNTHIA-LUCINDA[6] [344.] (Nathaniel[5], Jr., Nathaniel[4], Richard[3], Serjt. John[2], Thomas[1]), lived in Williston, Vt., where she died. She married, May 25, 1828, NA-
THANIEL PARKER, son of Daniel and Ann (Healey) Parker,
born in Salisbury, N. H., Jan. 31, 1807 ; he now lives in Burlington, Vt. From 1843 to 1849 he was Deputy Collector of
Customs ; retired from active business about 1870, and since
then was for six years Assistant Judge of County Court. He
married, 2, Jan. 15, 1846, Julia-Ann Haswell, born May 3,
1818, a daughter of Nathan-B. Haswell of Burlington, and
sister of Harriette-B. Haswell who married Julius-Otis Harris[6] [see Nos. 346, 360.]. Nathaniel and Cynthia-Lucinda
(Harris[6]) Parker had the following

357. Edwin-Ruthven [390.], b. Dec. 17, 1830, d. Nov. 11, 1848.
358. George-Harris, b. March 22, 1834, d. Sept. 11, 1836, in Williston.
359. Sarah [391.], b. Sept. 2, 1838.

360. JULIUS-OTIS[6] [346.] (Rufus[5], Nathaniel[4], Richard[3],
Serjt. John[2], Thomas[1]), was born in Bridport, Vt., May 1,
1808, and died in New Orleans, La., Dec. 23, 1869. He attended school in Bridport until the age of twelve or thirteen,
when he left school and entered a store as clerk ; was engaged in mercantile business most of his life. He left Vermont in 1830 and went to Mobile, Ala., and subsequently removed to New Orleans, previously spending six months in
Havana, Cuba, for his health. "He was gifted with a remarkably fine memory, particularly in connection with im-

portant political events. He wielded a ready pen, and was quite entertaining in conversation."

He possessed fine literary tastes, and wrote a great deal for the newspaper press. For two years—about 1838—he was commercial editor of the *Register and Enquirer* of Mobile, Ala. For seven years, from 1849 to 1856, he was a Director of Public Schools in New Orleans, during that time "constantly contributing short, fugitive articles to the different papers there, the *Picayune, Times,* and *Crescent.* He was deeply interested in the cause of education. A letter of his to the Mayor of Mobile, Ala., dated "New Orleans, May, 1849," and which was published in a newspaper, gives an account of the free public school system of the Second Municipality of New Orleans, with strong arguments in favor of free education. April 22, 1868, he was appointed by Hon. E. Heath, Mayor of New Orleans, to the duty of visiting and making a report of the various charitable institutions in the cities of New Orleans and Jefferson,—twenty-seven in number. This duty he completed and made his report June 9,—making a printed pamphlet of forty-four pages.

He was "an indefatigable member of the Howard Association" of New Orleans, "a body composed of thirty members, chartered by the State", whose object was the relief and care of the sick and suffering poor people in times of an epidemic of yellow fever or other disease. A New Orleans newspaper of Oct., 1847, in an article upon the "Howard Association" of that city, says:—"To these names [the officers of the Association] we can not forbear adding that of our friend, J.-O. Harris, of the commercial house of J.-O. & C.-E. Harris, who was a member of the committee to solicit contributions, and visit the sick and dying. It is to his exertions that much of the success attending the effort which was made in New York and other Northern cities, to increase the funds of the society, is to be attributed." An article written by Julius-O. Harris", published in the *Commercial Advertiser* of Mobile, and dated Sept., 1853, gives an extended and accurate account of "The Yellow Fever and the Howard Association" in New Orleans.

He married, Oct. 13, 1834, Harriette-Baldwin Haswell, daughter of Nathan-B. Haswell of Burlington, Vt., and sister to Julia-A. Haswell, who married Nathaniel Parker [see No. 356.]. She was born in Burlington, July 26, 1814, and now lives with her daughter and youngest son in Amite City, La.

CHILDREN.

361. Charles, b. March 31, 1836, in Mobile, Ala., d. Spring, 1843, in New Orleans.

362. Rosaline [393.], b. Aug. 9, 1838, in Mobile, Ala.

363. Otis [395.], b. July 22, 1840, in Mobile, Ala.

364. Haswell, b. Sept. 7, 1843, in Burlington, Vt., d. Oct. 1, 1870, in Burlington; was an invalid.

365. Joseph-Lyon [402.], b. Sept. 14, 1847, in Burlington, Vt.

366. CHARLES-EDWIN⁶ [347.] (Rufus⁵, Nathaniel⁴, Richard³, Serjt. John², Thomas¹), was born in Bridport, Vt., Oct. 1, 1810, and now resides in Philadelphia, Pa. He writes, April, 1881:—"I remained in Vermont until I was twenty-one, and then went South; was in New Orleans and Mobile for twenty years, and from thence went to New York City, where I remained ten years, and thence to this city (Philadelphia) where I have been for the past eighteen years; all this time (forty-eight years) have been engaged in the mercantile business." He married, Oct. 31, 1839, Mrs. Elizabeth-A. Sager, daughter of John-Francois David, born in Richmond, Va., Dec. 12, 1805, died in Philadelphia, Pa., Jan. 8, 1876. Her father was a native of Paris, France: he was killed in battle in the War of 1812.

CHILD, BORN IN MOBILE, ALA.

367. Mary-Clayes [403.], b. Feb. 9, 1841.

368. MARY-NIXON⁶ [349.] (Rufus⁵, Nathaniel⁴, Richard³, Serjt. John², Thomas¹), married, Sept. 12, 1843, Rev. Be-

THEL. FARRAND, a clergyman of the Presbyterian Church. He was the son of Samuel and Mary (Kitchel) Farrand, born in Addison, Vt., May 27, 1812; was educated at Middlebury College, Vt., graduating in 1839. He was ordained to the ministry by Rockaway Presbytery, N. J., in 1842; preached at Augusta and Branchville, N. J., also at La Fayette and Deckertown, N. J. In 1859 he removed with his family to Lima, Indiana, at which place he preached to a Presbyterian church, and to a Congregational church in Ontario, at the same time. He died in Ontario, Ind., May 7, 1866. Mrs. Farrand now resides with her daughter Mrs. A.-F. Chase, in Lake Stay, Minn.

CHILDREN.

369. Martha-Clayes [104.], b. Oct. 31, 1844, in Bridport, Vt., d. May 18, 1876.
370. Ellen-Sophia [108.], b. Nov. 25, 1847, in Augusta, N. J.
371. Caroline-Allen [110.], b. Aug. 13, 1857, in Deckertown, N. J.

372. HANNAH-ALMIRA⁶ [351.] (Richard⁵, Nathaniel⁴, Richard³, Serjt. John², Thomas¹), was born, lived, and died in Brandon, Vt.; married, Aug. 22, 1836, ALANSON DRAPER, a shoemaker. He was the son of James and Betsey (McNall) Draper, and was born in the east settlement of Argenteil, Province of Quebec, Feb. 9, 1809, and died in Brandon, Vt., May 11, 1875. Their children were all born in Brandon, except the oldest one, who was born in Lowell, Vt.

CHILDREN.

373. Lora-Melinda, b. Feb. 18, 1839, d. March 2, 1839, in Lowell, Vt.
374. William-Appleton, b. Nov. 15, 1842, d. June 3, 1843, in Brandon, Vt.
375. Julia-Eliza, b. Oct. 11, 1844, d. Oct. 8, 1848, in Brandon, Vt.
376. George-Harris [111.], b. Feb. 15, 1847.
377. Albert-James-Richard [113.], b. July 1, 1849.

378. BETSEY-MATILDA⁶ [352.] (Richard⁵, Nathaniel⁴, Richard³, Serjt. John², Thomas¹), was born and died in Brandon, Vt.; married, Feb. 11, 1832, MILO-ORLANDO MOTT, who was born in Enosburg, Vt., in 1808; was a boot

and shoe dealer in Brandon and elsewhere; and now resides in Springfield, Mass.

CHILDREN, BORN IN BRANDON, VT.

379. Julius-Harris [414.], b. May 26, 1836.
380. Charles-Appleton [418.], b. June 27, 1841.

381. SARAH-LOUISA[6] [353.] (Richard[5], Nathaniel[4], Richard[3], Serjt. John[2], Thomas[1]), married, Feb. 2, 1841, MARK BOWEN, a farmer, son of Jonathan and Esther (Stewart) Bowen; he was born in Royalton, Vt., May 23, 1810, and died in Royalton, Aug. 31, 1859. His widow lived for some time in Brandon, Vt., but now resides with her oldest daughter, Mrs. C.-F. Waldo, on the old homestead in Royalton.

CHILDREN, BORN IN ROYALTON, VT.

382. Fannie-Maria [422.], b. Nov. 11, 1841.
383. Caroline-Frances [426.], b. Jan. 16, 1843.
384. Louise [432.], b. Nov. 13, 1845.
385. Ella-Theresa, b. June 3, 1850, d. April 27, 1852.
386. Ella-Harris [441.], b. June 16, 1852.
387. Eugene-Stewart, b. March 20, 1854, d. Aug. 11, 1872.
388. Anna-Cora-Mowatt, b. April 7, 1857, d. Dec. 6, 1880.

389. LYDIA-GOODNOW[6] [355.] (Richard[5], Nathaniel[4], Richard[3], Serjt. John[2], Thomas[1]), was born and has always lived—with the exception of four years' absence—in Brandon, Vt. She married, Oct. 26, 1845, CHANCEY-LEE CASE, M. D. He was born July 7, 1819, in Fairfield, Vt., in the same school district where President Arthur was born, whose family were his next door neighbors, and whose sisters were his schoolmates. At the age of twelve he was a pupil of Rev. William Arthur, father of the President; was precocious in work, study and music; recited Murray's Grammar flippantly at eight, outdid all the members of the Sabbath school in learning verses, and at twelve played on a fiddle of his own construction. He obtained an education under great difficulties, studied medicine, graduating in the fall of 1845.

He practiced medicine nearly five years, when, his health failing, he started the old Brandon Drug Store in 1850, and carried on a successful business for twenty-five years, running a second store in Middlebury, Vt., for six years.

He was town Superintendant of Schools seven years, and a director in the First National Bank of Brandon twelve years; for ten years correspondant of the daily Rutland, Vt. *Herald*, and an occasional contributor to other papers, and has written and delivered a number of lectures. He has a library of five hundred volumes. Articles of his concerning the birth and early life of President Arthur were widely copied. He was the chief witness in disproving the story that the President was born in Canada. Dr. Case has been prominent in musical affairs; has conducted many choirs, and has been organist of the Baptist church for twenty-one years; was president of the Western Vermont Musical Association four years. He has retired from active business life; they reside in Brandon, Vt.

SEVENTH GENERATION.

390. EDWIN-RUTHVEN PARKER⁷ [357.] (Cynthia-Lucinda⁶ (Parker), Nathaniel⁵, Jr., Nathaniel⁴, Richard³, Serjt. John², Thomas¹), was a very promising young man and a remarkably fine scholar. He fitted for college at the Williston, Vt. Academy, and entered the University of Vermont at Burlington in Sept., 1846, before he was sixteen years of age. He intended after graduating there to pursue his studies in the Law School of Harvard University, but did not live to carry out his plans. He died in Burlington, Vt., Nov. 11, 1848, aged 18.

391. SARAH PARKER⁷ [359.] (Cynthia-Lucinda⁶ (Parker), Nathaniel⁵, Jr., Nathaniel⁴, Richard³, Serjt. John², Thomas¹), married, Jan. 22, 1862, CLARK NELLIS, a native of St. Johnsville, N. Y., who lived in Burlington, Vt., and was engaged in the wholesale and retail furniture business,

and wholesale and retail crockery business. He died July 9, 1875, and Mrs. Nellis and her son live with her father, Nathaniel Parker, in Burlington.

392. Walter-Parker, b. Dec. 18, 1862; is engaged in the lumber business in Burlington, in the employ of Sheppard & Morse.

393. ROSALINE⁷ [362.] (Julius-Otis⁶, Rufus⁵, Nathaniel⁴, Richard³, Serjt. John², Thomas¹), graduated at the High School in New Orleans, La., in Dec., 1855, and since the age of nineteen has been engaged in teaching; is at present first assistant—having charge of the intermediate department —in the Gullett Institute in Amite City, La. She has written articles for the children's department of *The Southern Plantation* (Montgomery, Ala.), and the Amite City *Independent*, using the signature "Daisy Dewdrop". She married, May 11, 1876, HEZEKIAH-AYER SWASEY, M. D. He was born in St. Johnsbury, Vt., Dec. 9, 1824, attended the University of Vermont, removed to Farmington, Iowa, at the age of thirteen, and graduated at the Medical School in Cincinnati, O. He was all his life devoted to literary pursuits, and all branches of horticulture and pomology; was a gentleman of rare literary accomplishments, having the reputation of being "the best botanist in Louisiana, one of the finest pomologists in the United States, and one of the most elegant writers in the South". He was at different times editor of many agricultural journals in Mississippi, Alabama, and Louisiana, among them *The Southern Plantation* (Montgomery, Ala.), *Our Home Journal* (New Orleans, La.), and *Swasey's Southern Gardener* (Tangipahoa, La.). Dr. Swasey married twice. After his second marriage in 1876, he settled in Tangipahoa, La., and resumed the practice of his profession. "Much of Southern agricultural and horticultural knowledge is due to his earnest and unselfish labors." He died in Tangipahoa, Sept. 18, 1878, leaving four daugh-

ters by his first wife, and by his second, Rosaline (Harris'), the following

394. Haswell-Aubrey, b. May 11, 1877.

395. Otis' [363.] (Julius-Otis[6], Rufus[5], Nathaniel[4], Richard[3], Serjt. John[2], Thomas[1]), graduated at the High School in New Orleans, La., in Dec., 1855, at the age of fifteen; then attended the Academy and then the University of Vermont at Burlington, Vt., returning to New Orleans after remaining in the latter institution three months, and entering the employ of a wholesale grocer, with whom he remained a number of years. For about eighteen months during the Civil war he held the position of Acting Assistant Adjutant General on the staff of Gen. D.-H. Maury, commanding the Department of the Gulf at Mobile, Ala. He is a book-keeper, "said to possess superior qualifications in his line of business," and at different times has been in the employ of various firms in New Orleans and in Texas. Since May, 1877, he has been book-keeper for F.-F. Hansell, stationer, publisher, and dealer in law books, in New Orleans. He is Past Grand Worthy Chief for the State of Louisiana, of the Order of Knights of Temperance; also is Senior Past Grand Dictator for the State of Louisiana, of the Order of Knights of Honor. He married, May 19, 1869, Kate O'Neil, daughter of Thomas and Mary-Ann (Burke) O'Neil, born in New Orleans, Dec. 28, 1846. Three of their children died of yellow fever in New Orleans, in the summer of 1878.

CHILDREN.

396. Thomas-Otis, b. March 27, 1870, in New Orleans, La.
397. Augustus-Block, b. Dec. 24, 1871, in Corsicana, Tex.
398. Iola-Alexine, b. Nov. 9, 1873, in Dallas, Tex., d. Aug. 31, 1878.
399. Richard-O'Neil, b. Jan. 13, 1875, in New Orleans, d. Sept. 3, 1878.
400. Albert-Omega, b. Dec. 24, 1877, in New Orleans, d. June 19, 1878.
401. Cary-Ivy, b. Sept. 1, 1879, in New Orleans.

402. Joseph-Lyon' [365.] (Julius-Otis[6], Rufus[5], Nathan-

iel[4], Richard[3], Serjt. John[2], Thomas[1]), became blind at the age of seven; the cause was not known, but supposed to have been a partial sunstroke.   He was educated at the Perkins Institute for the Blind, in Boston, Mass.; subsequently perfected himself in the art of piano tuning at the Institute for the Blind, Baton Rouge, La., finishing the course in July, 1880.   He resides in Amite City, La.

403.   MARY-CLAYES[7] [367.] (Charles-Edwin[6], Rufus[5], Nathaniel[4], Richard[3], Serjt. John[2], Thomas[1]), was educated at Mrs. Mears' Seminary, New York, completing the course in 1859.   She lives with her father in Philadelphia, Pa., and is engaged in teaching private pupils in vocal and instrumental (piano) music.

404.   MARTHA-CLAYES FARRAND[7] [369.] (Mary-Nixon[6] (Farrand), Rufus[5], Nathaniel[4], Richard[3], Serjt. John[2], Thomas[1]), received an excellent education, pursuing her studies with her father and at the La Grange Collegiate Institute in Indiana, afterwards teaching in this institution. "She possessed rare mental powers, was a *natural* teacher, and a facile writer". She wrote for various papers, principally for the *Advance* (Chicago), and the *Herald and Presbyter* (Cincinnati).   She married, Sept. 18, 1866, CHARLES-LEANDER DOOLITTLE, born in Ontario, Ind., Nov. 12, 1843; he was educated at Michigan University, Ann Arbor, where he graduated as Civil Engineer in June, 1874; was for some time in government service, and has been, since the summer of 1875, Professor of Astronomy and Mathematics in Lehigh University, South Bethlehem, Pa.   He removed in 1875 to South Bethlehem, where his wife died the next year.

CHILDREN.

405.   Alfred, b. June 14, 1867, in Ontario, Ind.
406.   Eric, b. July 26, 1870, in Ontario, Ind.
407.   Alice-Farrand, b. May 17, 1876, in South Bethlehem, Pa., d. Aug. 24, 1876, in Ontario, Ind.

408.   ELLEN-SOPHIA FARRAND[7] [370.] (Mary-Nixon[6]

(Farrand), Rufus⁵, Nathaniel⁴, Richard³, Serjt. John², Thomas¹), attended the La Grange Collegiate Institute in Indiana, and graduated in July, 1868 at Coldwater Female Seminary in Michigan. She taught school; married, Aug. 21, 1874, ALLEN-FLETCHER CHASE, a farmer; they reside in Lake Stay, Lincoln Co., Minn.

CHILD, BORN IN ONTARIO, IND.

469. John-Bethuel, b. Feb. 17, 1876.

410. CAROLINE-ALLEN FARRAND⁷ [371.] (Mary-Nixon⁶ (Farrand), Rufus⁵, Nathaniel⁴, Richard³, Serjt. John², Thomas¹), attended the La Grange Collegiate Institute in Indiana for some years, and in 1875 entered Bishop Thorpe School (an Episcopal female seminary) at South Bethlehem, Pa. From the fall of 1876 until 1880 she was employed as teacher in the public schools of Bethlehem, Pa. In Sept., 1880 she went to Utah as a missionary teacher under the care of the Presbyterian Board of Home Missions. She writes:—"I was located first at Manti, in the San Pete region of southern Utah, one hundred and fifty miles south of Salt Lake City, —the land of sage-brush, Mormons, and Indians. There are a minister and teacher at Manti, the only 'Gentiles' in the place. The inhabitants are principally Danes and Norwegians, from the peasantry." She left Manti in Jan., 1881, and in March was sent to Malad City, Idaho,—fifty miles from the railroad—to open the missionary work there, the people being Mormons or apostates, and mostly Welsh. She says: —"I began teaching in March with five pupils, and closed my first term in June with thirty-one, and have a Sabbath school [July, 1881,] of fifty members." The schools were held in a little log-cabin in which she also lived. In Jan., 1882, she gave up her mission work, and was succeeded by Rev. E.-M. KNOX and wife. Some of her writings have been published in different periodicals. She married, Oct. 23, 1881, JOHN-M. MORGAN, of Malad City; they live on a ranch or farm two miles south of Malad City, Idaho.

411.   GEORGE-HARRIS DRAPER[7] [376.] (Hannah-Almira[6]
(Draper), Richard[5], Nathaniel[4], Richard[3], Serjt. John[2],
Thomas[1]), is a farmer: went to Illinois, then to Kansas in
April, 1878, and in the spring of 1882 settled in Planking-
ton, Aurora Co., Dakota, where he now resides.   He mar-
ried, Oct. 2, 1876, Angelina-P. Runnion, born in Norfolk,
St. Lawrence Co., N. Y., April 11, 1848.

CHILD, BORN IN GREELEY, KANSAS.

412. George-Albert, b. Jan. 8, 1881.

413.   ALBERT-JAMES-RICHARD DRAPER[7] [377.] (Hannah-
Almira[6] (Draper), Richard[5], Nathaniel[4], Richard[3], Serjt.
John[2], Thomas[1]), is a dealer in "harnesses, whips, robes,
blankets, and everything in the horse clothing line", in Brandon, Vt.   He married, April 8, 1872, Mary-Jane Smith of
Brandon, daughter of John and Mary (Howard) Smith, born
in Richford, Vt., March 18, 1849.

414.   JULIUS-HARRIS MOTT[7] [379.]   (Betsey-Matilda[6]
(Mott), Richard[5], Nathaniel[4], Richard[3], Serjt. John[2], Thomas[1]), is partner in the Storage Warehouse firm of J.-H.
Mott & Co., in San Francisco, Cal., where he resides.   He
married, June 9, 1862, Ellen-Ada Cogswell of East Middlebury, Vt., daughter of Eber-E. and Sarah (Heath) Cogswell, born Dec. 21, 1835, and died in Sonora, Tuolumne Co.,
Cal., Aug. 21, 1875.   Their children are now living with her
father, Eber-E. Cogswell, in East Middlebury.

CHILDREN.

415.   Ernest-Julian, b. Sept. 27, 1865, in East Middlebury, Vt.
416.   Stella-Hosmer, b. Aug. 28, 1868, in Washington, D. C.
417.   Leslie-Cornell, b. Sept. 4, 1872, in Oakland, Cal.

418.   CHARLES-APPLETON MOTT[7] [380.] (Betsey-Matilda[6] (Mott), Richard[5], Nathaniel[4], Richard[3], Serjt. John[2],
Thomas[1]), is a dealer in boots and shoes in Fitchburg, Mass.
He married, Nov. 14, 1865, Maggie Roy, daughter of Andrew and Margaret Roy of Walpole, N. H., born in Brookline, Mass., March 19, 1845.

CHILDREN.

419. Clifford-Harris, b. Oct. 19, 1866, in Bellows Falls, Vt.
420. Bertice-Elmer, b. May 2, 1873, in Fitchburg, Mass.
421. Lillian-Agnes, b. March 19, 1877, in Brandon, Vt.

422. FANNIE - MARIA BOWEN[7] [382.] (Sarah-Louisa[6] (Bowen), Richard[5], Nathaniel[4], Richard[3], Serjt. John[2], Thomas[1]), married, March 22, 1860, CHARLES-F. WALDO, a farmer; they live in Royalton, Vt. on "Maple Grove Farm", the homestead of Mrs. Waldo's parents.

CHILDREN, BORN IN ROYALTON, VT.

423. Nellie-Fannie, b. May 14, 1861, d. Sept. 7, 1863.
424. Charles-Edward, b. Aug. 29, 1864.
425. Willis-Clarence, b. Jan. 18, 1867.

426. CAROLINE-FRANCES BOWEN[7] [383.] (Sarah-Louisa[6] (Bowen), Richard[5], Nathaniel[4], Richard[3], Serjt. John[2], Thomas[1]), married, Dec. 25, 1862, LUKE-BOWEN FAIRBANKS, a farmer; they live in Rose Creek, Mower Co., Minn. He was in the Civil war; enlisted as a private in Co. F. 3rd Regiment Vermont Volunteers, and was mustered into service, July 16, 1861. He was wounded at Lee's Mills, Va., April 16, 1862; re-enlisted as veteran Dec. 22, 1863. He was promoted from Serjeant to First Lieutenant of Co. H, and mustered in July 24, 1864; promoted to Captain of Co. C, and mustered in Oct. 8, 1864; discharged and mustered out of service, July 11, 1865.

CHILDREN.

427. Samuel-Pingree, b. April 29, 1866.
428. Henry-Durant, b. April 13, 1869.
429. Eugene-Stewart, b. Feb. 14, 1871.
430. Guy-Luke, b. July 1, 1873.
431. Dan, b. Sept. 30, 1877.

432. LOUISE BOWEN[7] [384.] (Sarah-Louisa[6] (Bowen), Richard[5], Nathaniel[4], Richard[3], Serjt. John[2], Thomas[1]), married, Dec. 25, 1865, DAVID-E. BALLARD; they reside in Barnes, Washington Co., Kansas. He was a member of the first State Legislature of Kansas in 1861, representing Wash-

ington County ; was also a Representative in the Legislatures
of 1867 and 1879.   He was in the Civil war ; was First
Lieutenant in the 2nd Regiment Kansas Cavalry from Jan.
10, 1862 to Feb. 15, 1865.   From the latter date to Dec. 31,
1866, he was Quartermaster-general of the State of Kansas.
In 1868 and 1869 he was Assistant Assessor of United States
Internal Revenue, for the Fourth District of Kansas. In 1872
and 1873 he was Railroad Assessor of the Twelfth District
of Kansas.

CHILDREN.

433. Ernest-Frederick, b. Dec. 22, 1866.
434. Louise, b. June 16, 1868, d. June 22, 1868.
435. Frank-Crosby, b. July 14, 1869.
436. Mabel, b. Sept. 9, 1871.
437. Miriam, b. Sept. 12, 1873.
438. David-Chaney-Case, b. Nov. 7, 1875.
439. Winifred, b. Nov. 27, 1877.
440. Mark-Appleton, b. Dec. 29, 1880.

441.   ELLA-HARRIS BOWEN⁷ [386.] (Sarah-Louisa⁶ (Bowen), Richard⁵, Nathaniel⁴, Richard³, Serjt. John², Thomas¹),
married, March 18, 1874, WILLIAM McFARLAND, a farmer :
they live in Rose Creek, Mower County, Minn.

CHILDREN.

442. Mark-Bowen, b. Dec. 18, 1874, in Windom, Minn.
443. Albert-John, b. Jan. 18, 1878, in Nevada, Minn.

CHAPTER X.

444. WILLIAM HARRIS[4] [11.] (Richard[3], Serjt. John[2],
Thomas[1]), the youngest of the family, was born in Harvard,
Mass., Oct. 8, 1754; baptized there Oct. 13; died in Grafton, Vermont, August 30, 1831. "He was in the war of the
Revolution, through the war, or seven years: was in the battle of Bunker Hill: he lost his health, but did not get a
scar." It is said that he was taken prisoner by the British
and roughly treated. "It has been said that he was the man
that sewed the gold buttons on to Washington's coat." On
the Massachusetts Revolutionary Rolls William Harris of
Harvard is credited as follows:—

Vol. 12: 199. 8 days' service on Lexington Alarm, from
April 26, 1775, and "enlisted in the army."

Cont. Rolls. 8 months' service in Burt's Co., Whitcomb's
Regiment, 1775.

Cont. Army Books. 3 years' service, Capt. Brown's Co.,
M. Jackson's 8th Regiment, from April 1, 1777 to April 1,
1780.

He settled in Grafton, Vermont, previous to 1786, where
all his children were born. He was one of the first settlers
of that town: cleared up a farm, and lived in a log house.
He bought from Aaron Putnam 120 acres of land, Lot 9,
Second Range, in Thomlinson—the early name of Grafton—

conveyed by deed dated May 25, 1781. He was then "of Rockingham, Vt." a town adjoining Grafton. He was a farmer; the farm he lived on is in the south part of the town of Grafton, and is now occupied by George Whitcomb. William Harris' was baptized and received into the (Calvinistic) Baptist church in Grafton in 1803, his wife joining the same year. In 1814 he was chosen Deacon of the church, which office he held until death.* A large proportion of his descendants have been Baptists in religious preference. His children were all members of Baptist churches, four belonging to the church in Grafton, with which church seven children of his son Jasher⁵ also united. He married Ruth Wetherby, who died in Grafton, May 27, 1833, aged 76.

CHILDREN, BORN IN GRAFTON, VT.

445. William [450.], b. Jan. 14, 1786, d. Dec. 8, 1847.
446. Martha, d. July 6, 1831, in Grafton, aged about 44.
447. Jasher [459.], b. April 6, 1790, d. April 18, 1866.
448. John-Wetherby [474.], b. Sept. 8, 1792, d. July 23, 1872.
449. Ruth [479.], b. Oct. 5, 1795, d. Oct. 28, 1858.

FIFTH GENERATION.

450. WILLIAM⁵, JUNIOR [445.] (Dea. William⁴, Richard³, Serjt. John², Thomas¹), was born in Grafton and died in Townshend, Vt. He was a member of the Baptist church in Grafton; was a farmer, and lived in Townshend, Vt., then called Acton. He married, Aug. 20, 1806, Lucretia Dennison, daughter of Amos Dennison of Grafton, Vt., born in Grafton, May 18, 1784, died in Townshend, April 27, 1837.

CHILDREN.

451. Roswell [489.], b. Nov. 7, 1806, d. April 12, 1855.
452. Billy, b. Dec. 12, 1807, in Grafton, Vt., d. March 12, 1808, in Grafton.
453. Abigail-Dennison [491.], b. April 16, 1809.
454. Lucius, b. Jan. 25, 1813, in Athens, Vt., d. April 3, 1813, in Athens.
455. Christopher [499.], b. March 12, 1814.

---

*Thus three of the four brothers were Deacons: William⁴ [No. 444.] a Baptist, and Jacob⁴ [see No. 17.] and Richard⁴, Jr. [see No. 141.] Congregationalists.

456.   Jonas [508.], b. May 11, 1816.
457.   Charles [512.], b. Nov. 18, 1822, d. March 30, 1870.
458.   John-Rollin, b. Sept. 7, 1826, in Townshend, Vt., d. Aug. 27, 1831, in T.

459.   JASHER⁵ [447.] (Dea. William⁴, Richard³, Serjt.
John², Thomas¹), spent his life in Grafton, Vt.; was born and
died there. He was a farmer and lived on the homestead
with his parents; was a member of the Baptist church in
Grafton. The accompanying portrait shows Jasher Harris'
at the age of seventy-five. He married, Dec. 1, 1814, Elizabeth Jordan, daughter of Sylvanus and Elizabeth (Hudson)
Jordan, born in Chesterfield, N. H., Jan. 11, 1795, and died
in Grafton, Jan. 16, 1845.

CHILDREN, BORN IN GRAFTON, VT.

460.   Daughter, d. in Grafton, aged three weeks.
461.   Sylvester [513.], b. Oct. 19, 1816, d. April 20, 1873.
462.   Marilla-Adaline [516.], b. Sept. 16, 1818.
463.   Mary, d. in Grafton, aged one year.
464.   Sarah, d. in Grafton, aged three years.
465.   Sylvanus, b. Nov. 1, 1824, d. Nov. 1, 1840, in Grafton.
466.   George-Washington [517.], b. Oct. 16, 1826.
467.   William-Randal [523.], b. Feb. 26, 1828.
468.   John-Marcus [524.], b. March 19, 1830.
469.   Mary-Ann, b. Dec. 10, 1831, d. March 22, 1878, in Lowell, Mass.
470.   Caroline-Matilda, b. Oct. 29, 1833, d. Aug. 22, 1878, in Lowell, Mass.
471.   Hubbard-Clinton [525.], b. Nov. 19, 1835.
472.   Francis-Tyler [530.], b. Sept. 21, 1837, d. Feb. 20, 1863.
473.   Sarah-Helen, b. July 17, 1839; lives in Lowell, Mass., with her brother
           George-W⁵.

474.   JOHN-WETHERBY⁵ [448.] (Dea. William⁴, Richard³,
Serjt. John², Thomas¹), was born in Grafton, and died in
Manchester, Vt. He lived in Grafton and farmed until April,
1822, then removing to Factory Point in Manchester, where
he lived the remainder of his life and carried on the business
of manufacturing broad-cloths. His two sons were in company with him, doing business under the firm name of J.-W.
Harris & Sons. They owned two factories in Manchester,
one at Factory Point, the other a mile and a half distant.
After the death of his sons the business was sold.   John.-W

Harris' was a fine singer, and in Grafton was in the habit of teaching district school in the winter and singing-school evenings; led the church choir in Factory Point for thirty years.

He had very firm anti-slavery principles, and voted that ticket when there were but eight cast in the town. He was Justice of the Peace over forty years; was a man of good judgment, was highly respected, and considered strictly honest at all times; a well-read man in religious matters, a strong Baptist, and very benevolent, assisting and caring for the poor and needy around him. He joined the (Calvinistic) Baptist church in Factory Point in August, 1838, and was clerk of the church from that time until his death. His wife was also a member. To the same church belonged their son Solon-H.[6] [see Nos. 475, 531,] and his wife, and *their* son John-W.[7], and his wife.

He married, in the spring of 1816, Mary Willey, daughter of Benjamin† and Abigail (Hurd) Willey, born in Goshen, N. H., June 6, 1795, died in Manchester, March 14, 1875, twenty years after the death of all her children.

CHILDREN.

475. Solon-Hurd [531.], b. Nov. 30, 1817, d. March 10, 1855.
476. Charles [533.], b. March 3, 1820, d. April 2, 1851.
477. Welthy, b. in Manchester, Vt., d. Jan., 1829, in M., in her fifth year.
478. Cornelia-Welthy, b. Nov. 15, 1829, in M., d. April 1, 1854, in M.

479. RUTH[5] [449,] (Dea. William[4], Richard[3], Serjt. John[2], Thomas[1]), was born, lived, and died in Grafton, Vt.; was a member of the Baptist church in that town. She married, May 5, 1814, HOSEA RHODES of Grafton, a farmer, son of Joseph and Mary Rhodes. He was born in Foxborough, Mass., March 10, 1787, and died in Marshalltown, Iowa, May 16, 1869. He married, 2, April 17, 1839, Mrs. Eliza-

*His father, Dea. William[4], was a singer.
†Benj. Willey, the youngest of four children, was born in Conn., April 16, 1760, died Aug. 19, 1823; he married, May 11, 1789, Abigail Hurd, the oldest of ten children, born in N. H., Nov. 26, 1769, died March 28, 1837; they removed to Grafton, Vt., in 1812.

beth Goodness, by whom he had no children.   She died Oct.
28, 1866.   In July, 1841 he removed with his family to Oberlin, Ohio, buying a farm two and one-half miles from the village, in Russia township.   Here he lived until a few years
before his death, when he removed to Marshalltown, Iowa.
Hosea and Ruth (Harris') Rhodes had the following

CHILDREN, BORN IN GRAFTON, VT.

480.   Maria, b. Dec. 24, 1846, d. Dec. 15, 1835, in Grafton.
481.   Son, b. Feb. 14, 1819, d. March, 1819, in Grafton, aged three weeks.
482.   Harriet-Mary [534.], b. Dec. 31, 1820.
483.   Abigail-Emily [535.], b. March 4, 1824, d. Sept. 24, 1858.
484.   Joseph, b. May 9, 1826, d. Oct., 1826, in Grafton.
485.   Solon-Harris [537.], b. Nov. 8, 1827, d. Aug. 29, 1879.
486.   Joseph-Warren [542.], b. Oct. 31, 1830, d. Dec. 29, 1879.
487.   William-Harris [549.], b. April 6, 1833, d. March 24, 1863.
488.   Isaac-Newton [552.], b. Feb. 12, 1837.

SIXTH GENERATION.

489.   ROSWELL[5] [451.] (William[5], Jr., Dea. William[4],
Richard[3], Serjt. John[2], Thomas[1]), was born in Grafton, Vt.
He was a brick-maker and lived in Coeymans, N. Y. (twelve
miles from Albany): was drowned in the Hudson river April
12, 1835, under the following circumstances:—"He left
the shore at Coeymans landing in company with another man
in a small row-boat, intending to get aboard a schooner
which was passing up the river, to go to Albany: on reach-
ing the schooner there was a collision, the small boat was up-
set and he was thrown into the river and drowned: his body
was not recovered until it had lain in the water thirty-six
days: his companion was saved." He married, Nov. 6, 1830,
Avis Sherman, daughter of Joseph and Sally (Gardner)
Sherman.   She was born in Somerset, R. I., Sept. 15, 1813,
and now lives with her daughter in Victory, N. Y.

CHILD, BORN IN COEYMANS, N. Y.

490.   Catharine-Elizabeth [555.], b. April 7, 1833.

491.   ABIGAIL-DENNISON[6] [453.] (William[5], Jr., Dea.
William[4], Richard[3], Serjt. John[2], Thomas[1]), was born in

Grafton, Vt.; married, 1, 1830, HIRAM WHITE, son of Josiah and Hannah White, born in Putney, Vt., May 6, 1796, died in Townshend, Vt., June 28, 1850. He was a farmer; they lived in Putney until the spring of 1840, then removed to Townshend, where they lived until his death.

CHILDREN.

492. Abby-Arabella [562.], b. July 7, 1831, in Langdon, N. H.
493. Newel-Hiram [565.], b. Feb. 12, 1833, in Putney, Vt.
494. Wealthy-Isabella [567.], b. April 19, 1835, in Putney, Vt.
495. Rollin-Charles [571.], b. June 3, 1837, in Putney, Vt.
496. Ruth-Ann, b. Oct. 5, 1840, in Townshend, Vt.
497. Lucretia-Catherine [574.], b. Oct. 27, 1845, in Townshend, Vt.
498. Fannie-Ella [580.], b. July 4, 1848, in Townshend, Vt.

She married, 2, August, 1855, JOHN-D. GATES of Grafton, Vt., a farmer, born in Townshend, died in Grafton, 1862. She has lived in Fitchburg, Mass., since 1871, with her daughter Ruth-Ann White⁷ [see No. 496.], who has resided there since 1859.

499. CHRISTOPHER⁶ [455.] (William⁵, Jr., Dea. William⁴, Richard⁵, Serjt. John², Thomas¹), was born in Athens, Vt.; lives in Martville, Cayuga Co., N. Y.; is a farmer and shoe-dealer. He married, 1, Nov. 11, 1838, Achsah Holden, daughter of Dennis and Achsah (Gates) Holden. She was born Jan. 14, 1816, in Townshend, Vt. (then Acton), and died in Townshend, July 29, 1855.

CHILDREN, BORN IN TOWNSHEND, VT.

500. Rollin-Roswell [584.], b. Sept. 28, 1839.
501. James-Oscar, b. Nov. 28, 1840, d. March 8, 1841.
502. Romanzo-Altheron [588.], b. Sept. 9, 1842.
503. Avis-Fidelia [590.], b. Oct. 29, 1843.
504. Alzamon-Redinton, b. March 13, 1847, d. Sept. 22, 1848.
505. Achsah-Celestia [597.], b. July 19, 1849.
506. Orange-Westopher, b. June 25, 1854, d. Aug. 4, 1855.

He married, 2, Feb. 17, 1856, Elvira-C. Holden of Townshend, born Jan. 13, 1830, with whom he lived about seven years. He married, 3, Nov. 28, 1865, Harriet-T. Liddle.

CHILD, BORN IN MARTVILLE, N. Y.

507. Burdett, b. Jan. 28, 1868.

508. JONAS⁶ [456.] (William⁵, Jr., Dea. William⁴, Richard³, Serjt. John², Thomas¹), was born in Townshend, Vt., and now lives in the village of Westminster, Vt.; is a farmer. He married, Oct. 18, 1812, Octavia Goodridge of Westminster, and settled on her father's farm in that town, afterwards removing into the village.

CHILDREN, BORN IN WESTMINSTER, VT.

509. Loren-Goodridge, b. Aug. 6, 1843, d. Sept. 2, 1847.
510. Cemantha-Octavia, b. Sept. 24, 1848; lives with her parents.
511. Fred-Austin, b. Jan. 12, 1860; is a farmer; lives with his parents.

512. CHARLES⁶ [457.] (William⁵, Jr., Dea. William⁴, Richard³, Serjt. John², Thomas¹), born in Townshend, Vt., was a carpenter working on railroads and lived in various places. "He was in the South when the Civil war broke out, and was forced into the Confederate army, and lost everything that he had—some two thousand dollars—when he went South. He was taken prisoner at the battle of Vicksburg, and imprisoned at Camp Morton, Indianapolis, Ind." He then wrote to his brother Jonas⁶ [see No. 508,] to help him out, and after two or three applications to the government and after long delay he was released, and took the oath of allegiance. He went to his brother's in Westminster, Vt., arriving there "with his prison suit on, with frozen feet, hands and limbs. Several months later he started to work his way back to the South to see if he could regain anything, but he got only as far as Philadelphia, Pa., when he was taken sick, and died March 30, 1870."

513. SYLVESTER⁶ [461.] (Jasher⁵, Dea. William⁴, Richard³, Serjt. John², Thomas¹), was born in Grafton, Vt., where his youth and early manhood were spent; in the spring of 1845 he removed to Coeymans, Albany Co., N. Y., where he spent the remainder of his life, and where he died. He was engaged in the manufacture of brick, afterwards in farming, and during the last few years of his life raised broom-corn and manufactured brooms. "He was a hard-working and

very industrious business man, and had the entire confidence
and respect of the whole community in which he lived. He
was a conscientious Christian, a man of perfect truth and integrity, and one who was true to every duty in life, and faithful to every trust, and who endeared himself to all who knew
him." He married, May 18, 1851, Mary Clement, daughter of Moses Clement, M. D., who was "one of the most
honored citizens of Coeymans" [see No. 524.]. She was
born in Coeymans, Feb. 9, 1818, and died there Dec. 23,
1880.

CHILDREN, BORN IN COEYMANS, N. Y.

514. Julia-Estelle [601.], b. Dec. 25, 1853.
515. Moses-Clement [605.], b. May 7, 1856, d. April 15, 1881.

516. MARILLA-ADALINE⁶ [462.] (Jasher⁵, Dea. William⁴,
Richard³, Serjt. John², Thomas¹), married, Feb. 22, 1866,
EPHRAIM WILBUR of Grafton, Vt., a farmer, son of Field
and Martha (Burt) Wilbur, born in Norton, Mass. She was
the only one of her father's large family who remained in
Vermont. Mr. Wilbur died in Grafton, Sept. 5, 1875; he
had three children by a former wife, one of whom, Vestus-A.,
lives with Mrs. Wilbur in Grafton, and another, Vesta-A.,
married George Whitcomb and lives on the old homestead of
Dea. William Harris¹ [see No. 414.].

517. GEORGE-WASHINGTON⁶ [466.] (Jasher⁵, Dea. William⁴, Richard³, Serjt. John², Thomas¹), was born in Grafton, Vt., Oct. 16, 1826, and now resides in Lowell, Mass.
"He attended for several terms the Academy at Townshend,
Vt., and at the age of fifteen began to teach school, which he
continued for three years. In 1845 he invented a machine for
making brick, and employed his summer vacation in pursuing this industry and in making and selling his machines.
His attention being called to the need of a loom-harness machine, he set to work with the purpose of devising one, and
finally succeeded, taking out a patent for such a machine in
1849. After teaching a year at Elizabeth, N. J., he returned

to Grafton and for the next five or six years devoted himself to improving his invention. He went to England in 1859, with the design of establishing a business in that country, where he remained for six months. Soon after his return he took three of his machines to Lowell, Mass., rented the basement of a shop and began the manufacture of twine loom harness, continuing in this about a year, when the outbreak of the Civil war, by closing the cotton mills, cut off his business. Six months later some of the mills in the manufacturing cities had started up, and Mr. Harris rented room and power and again began operations. He gradually added to the number of his machines and operatives, and in 1872 leased land and erected a three-story building, which he occupied until April, 1881, when it was destroyed by fire. Taking what machines he could use after the fire he rented rooms for his business while erecting at the corner of Pawtucket and Perkins streets a four-story brick building, 150 by 50 feet in size, of which he occupies the first two floors, and which was completed in Nov., 1881. A view of this factory is here inserted.

He is now running 25 machines, employing 35 hands, and annually producing about 45,000 sets of twine loom harness, consuming 175,000 pounds of twine.

"Besides this business Mr. Harris formed a partnership in 1867 with W.-W. Carey for the manufacture of wood-working machinery. They erected a two-story brick machine shop, and are now manufacturing planers, saws, wood-turning lathes, and various other machines. Mr. Harris has one-fourth interest in the Swaine Turbine Company, of which he was formerly president, and is still a director. He, with four others, established the Lake George Manufacturing Company of Ticonderoga, N. Y., with 10,000 spindles and 250 looms, of which he was one-third owner and president, the annual production being 52,000 yards of sheeting, employing 200 hands." See portrait.

He married, 1, Dec. 4, 1855, Susan Wier, daughter of John and Fannie (Chapman) Wier, born in Grafton, Vt., Dec. 4, 1828, and died in Lowell, Mass., March 12, 1866.

CHILDREN.

518. Rosetta-Caroline, b. Aug. 9, 1858, in Coeymans, N. Y., d. March 7, 1859, in Coeymans.
519. Emma-Susan, b. Feb. 1, 1862, in Lowell, Mass., d. Jan. 29, 1880, in Grafton, Vt.; buried on her eighteenth birthday.
520. Sarah-Helen, b. Sept. 7, 1863, in Lowell, d. Dec. 5, 1881, in Lowell.
521. George-William, b. Feb. 9, 1866, in Lowell.

He married, 2, Dec. 7, 1870, Emma-Roslyn Lunt, daughter of Joseph and Sarah (Johnson) Lunt, born in Brunswick, Me., May 12, 1845.

CHILD, BORN IN LOWELL, MASS.

522. Grace-Greenleaf, b. Oct. 12, 1872.

523. WILLIAM-RANDAL[6] [167.] (Jasher[5], Dea. William[4], Richard[3], Serjt. John[2], Thomas[1]), went to Europe in 1851, and is engaged in the manufacture of loom harness in Manchester, England. He married Margaret Thackeray, an English lady, but has no children except one adopted daughter.

524. JOHN-MARCUS[6] [468.] (Jasher[5], Dea. William[4], Richard[3], Serjt. John[2], Thomas[1]), was born in Grafton, Vt.; at-

John-S. and Laura (Graves) Pettibone. She was born Jan., 1821, and died in Manchester, Sept. 25, 1852.

531. HARRIET-MARY RHODES[6] [482.] (Ruth[5] (Rhodes), Dea. William[4], Richard[3], Serjt. John[2], Thomas[1]), was born in Grafton, Vt.; her father with his family removed to Oberlin, O., in 1841. She married, July 4, 1847, WILLIAM-M. LOREE, son of John and Abbie Loree, born in Morristown, N. J., Oct. 3, 1810. He married, 1, Oct., 1832, Frances-Maria Butler, who died Aug. 18, 1837. They had three children, William-Martin now of Vinton, Iowa, Andrew-Mulford now of Marshalltown, Iowa, and James-K.-Polk who died young. Mr. Loree was engaged in manufacturing woolens in Pittsfield, Mass., several years. In the fall of 1839 he removed to Medina, Ohio, living on a farm. In two or three years a railroad was surveyed across his farm, bringing up the price of land so that he sold and commenced again in the manufacturing business. In 1847 he married, 2, Harriet-Mary Rhodes[6]. In the spring of 1851 they removed to Columbus, O., and opened a grocery store and boarding-house, his oldest son being associated with him in the store. The son four years later removed to Vinton, Benton Co., Iowa, and the father sold out his business and removed to the same place in the spring of 1857. Here they have since resided; Mr. Loree has retired from active business life. In the fall of 1882 they visited their relatives in the East, and Mrs. Loree was enabled to revisit for the first time her native valley and the scenes of her early life in Grafton, Vt., which she had left more than forty years before. See portraits.

535. ABIGAIL-EMILY RHODES[6] [483.] (Ruth[5] (Rhodes), Dea. William[4], Richard[3], Serjt. John[2], Thomas[1]), commenced teaching school in Ohio in the summer of 1842, and taught several years; also taught painting and drawing. She married, March 21, 1856, DAVID McCLELLAND, and lived in Columbus, O., where she died in 1858. He was the son of George and Isabel (Leslie) McClelland, born in Portage Co.,

O., Feb. 19, 1824. In July, 1860, he went to the gold regions of Colorado and worked at mining. He was in the Civil war: enlisted Sept. 8, 1861 in Co. M, 1st Regiment Colorado Cavalry; was discharged from service April 5, 1864, but had re-enlisted Jan. 1, in the 1st veteran battalion Colorado Cavalry: was mustered out of service Oct. 30, 1865, on a general order owing to the close of the war. Since that time he has resided in Utica, Licking Co., O.: is a carriage-maker.

CHILD, BORN IN COLUMBUS, OHIO.

536. Edwin-David, b. June 18, 1858, d. Aug. 11, 1859, in Utica, O.

537. SOLON-HARRIS RHODES[6] [185.] (Ruth[5] (Rhodes), Dea. William[4], Richard[3], Serjt. John[2], Thomas[1]), was a farmer: lived in Russia township, Ohio, near Oberlin village, and died there. He was a sub-school director for nineteen years out of the last twenty before his death. He was president of a stock grocery company in Elyria, O. in 1876, and was elected director in a similar company in Oberlin in 1878: was a man of rare business qualities, strictly honest, and of excellent character and great usefulness in the community. A neighbor and friend of Mr. Rhodes writes :—

"He was such a model of morality and uprightness that his unconverted neighbors used to hold him up as a man who had no need of a change of heart to make him all that he ought to be in all the relations of life. And indeed he was of the same opinion until he was about forty years of age. Then a merciful God through the agency of the Holy Spirit lifted the veil that hides us from our own hearts and caused him to see that his own 'righteousness was as filthy rags'. After a mental struggle and conflict with the Powers of Darkness such as perhaps few pass through, he came out with 'flying colors', for Jesus Christ was the Captain of his salvation: and from that time till his death he was always at his post. He used to say 'I am amazed at myself that I could try to live a Christian for forty years without Christ.'"

Mr. Rhodes and his wife were among the twenty-four who in 1868 formed the Unity Church of School District No. 4 in Russia—a union Evangelical church. "He was a working Christian, and won the respect and esteem of all with whom he was acquainted." He married, Aug. 24, 1854, Mrs. Caroline-A. Lampman, widow of Charles Lampman. Caroline-A. Squire, daughter of William and Lorana (Buckingham) Squire [see No. 542.], married, 1, Feb. 11, 1849, Charles Lampman, and had one child, Mary-A., born in Elyria, O. She married, 2, Solon-Harris Rhodes[6], and now lives with her sons on the homestead near Oberlin.

CHILDREN, BORN IN RUSSIA, OHIO.

538.   Lillie-Lenora [612.], b. Aug. 31, 1857.
539.   Francis-Newton, b. March 10, 1859; is a farmer.
540.   Charles-Harris, b. May 23, 1861; is a farmer.
541.   Solon-Arthur, b. Jan. 2, 1864.

542.   JOSEPH-WARREN RHODES[6] [486.] (Ruth[5] (Rhodes), Dea. William[4], Richard[3], Serjt. John[2], Thomas[1]), was a farmer, but worked at the carpenter's trade a number of years; lived in Ohio until the fall of 1861, when he removed to Joyfield, Benzie Co., Michigan, bought a farm and lived there until his death, which occurred there. He was treasurer of Joyfield for about nine years, and school director three or four years, also township assessor. He married, Nov. 21, 1853, Mary-Nancy Squire, daughter of William and Lorana (Buckingham) Squire, born in Elyria, O., June 30, 1833. She is a sister to Caroline-A. Squire, who married Solon-H. Rhodes[6] [see No. 537.]. She married, 2, July 3, 1882, Alvah-Charles Acha, and now lives in Onekama, Manistee Co., Mich. Joseph-W[6]. and Mary-N. (Squire) Rhodes had the following

CHILDREN.

543.   Alice-Eugenie, b. Aug. 13, 1854, in Russia, O.; lives in Joyfield, Mich.
544.   Josephine-Adelaide, b. May 13, 1857, in Russia, O.; d. Feb. 7, 1858, in Elyria, O.

545. Josephine-Abbie [615.], b. Jan. 28, 1859, in Carlisle, O.
546. Hattie-Lorana, b. June 21, 1861, in Russia, O.; lives in Joyfield, Mich.
547. George-Harris, b. April 3, 1864, in Elyria, O.; lives in Joyfield, Mich.
548. Lucy-Adelaide, b. Nov. 1, 1867, in Joyfield, Mich.

549. WILLIAM-HARRIS RHODES⁶ [487.] (Ruth⁵ (Rhodes), Dea. William⁴, Richard³, Serjt. John², Thomas¹), was for several years engaged in the sale of books in company with his brother Isaac-Newton⁶ [see No. 552.], traveling in the South and employing several agents. The outbreak of the Civil war stopped their business and caused quite a loss of goods. At the time of his death in the spring of 1863 he had charge of a wholesale stationery and notion store in Nashville, Tenn., employed by a firm in Cincinnati, O.; his death occurred in Cincinnati. He was a man of much natural ability; was said to have inherited much from his mother; he possessed excellent business qualities, and had the prospect of a bright future before him at the time of his death. "He shrank not from duty, and deviated not a line from honor and integrity." See portrait.

He married, Sept. 16, 1858, Nettie-E. Fisk, a sister to Jane-H. Fisk [see No. 552.], born in Genesee, N. Y., Aug. 18, 1833. She married, 2, June 11, 1868, William-R. Tolles. He is a native of New Haven, Conn.; served through the Civil war, entering the service as Captain of an Ohio Company, and rising by promotions to the position of Colonel. They removed some years ago to San Bernardino, Cal., where they now reside; have one child, Lulu-M., born March 10, 1871. William-H.⁶ and Nettie-E. (Fisk) Rhodes had two

CHILDREN.

550. Daughter, b. Jan. 22, 1860, in Batesville, Ark., d. Jan. 22, 1860.
551. Minnie-Lara, b. Dec. 25, 1862, in Kalamazoo, Mich., d. April 8, 1869.

552. ISAAC-NEWTON RHODES⁶ [488.] (Ruth⁵ (Rhodes), Dea. William⁴, Richard³, Serjt. John², Thomas¹), attended the preparatory department of Oberlin College in the fall and

winter of 1854-5. In Dec., 1855 he engaged in the business of selling books, traveling in the Southern states; afterwards had charge of a portion of the business and employed agents. He was associated for several years with his brother William-H.[6] [see No. 549.] in this business. In 1861 he went to Lebanon, O. and attended three terms at the Normal School; taught school two winters, and in the spring of 1863 went to Nashville, Tenn. to take charge of the store where his brother William-H.[6] had been; remained there until the fall of 1865, then went to Chicago, Ill. and was employed as commercial salesman several years. In 1872 he engaged in the sale of sewing-machines in Marshalltown, Iowa, and in April, 1877 removed to Marysville, Cal., where he now resides and is engaged in the same business. He married, 1. June 11, 1868, Jane-H. Fisk, a sister to Nettie-E. Fisk, who married William-H. Rhodes[6] [see Nos. 487, 549.].

CHILDREN.

553. Mabel-Abbie, b. June 25, 1870, in Grinnell, Iowa.
554. William-Maxwell, b. Aug. 16, 1874, in Marshalltown, Iowa.

He married, 2. Dec. 27, 1884, Nellie-A. Bailey of San Jose, Cal.

SEVENTH GENERATION.

555. CATHARINE - ELIZABETH[6] [190.] (Roswell[6], William[5], Jr., Dea. William[4], Richard[3], Serjt. John[2], Thomas[1]), married, Jan. 11, 1853, ADDISON-BALDWIN WETHERBY, son of John and Sarah Wetherby, born in Victory, Cayuga Co., N. Y., Sept. 15, 1832. He is a merchant in Victory; has been postmaster for eighteen years, and Notary for District 24 for four years.

CHILDREN, BORN IN VICTORY, N. Y.

556. Ella-Harris [617.], b. April 1, 1854.
557. James-Roswell [649.], b. Feb. 17, 1856.
558. Clarence-Addison, b. June 1, 1858; is a farmer; lives with his parents.
559. Sarah-Eudora, b. Sept. 11, 1861, d. Sept. 17, 1865, in Victory.
560. Jennie-Elnora, b. Feb. 3, 1867, d. Sept. 30, 1869, in Victory.
561. Viola-Gertrude, b. Aug. 14, 1872.

562.   ABBY-ARABELLA WHITE[7] [492.] (Abigail-Dennison[6]
(White). William[5], Jr.. Dea. William[4], Richard[3], Serjt. John[2],
Thomas[1]), married, April 6, 1852, GEORGE WINSLOW, a
farmer, son of Peleg and Nancy (Bowles) Winslow.   He
was born in Dummerston, Vt., Feb. 7, 1827, lived in Townshend, Vt., where he died, Feb. 9, 1868.   His widow and
children reside in Townshend.

CHILDREN, BORN IN TOWNSHEND, VT.

563.   George-Peleg, b. Nov. 25, 1860; is a farmer.
564.   Fanny-Abby, b. Jan. 27, 1867.

565.   NEWEL-HIRAM WHITE[7] [493.] (Abigail-Dennison[6]
(White). William[5], Jr.. Dea. William[4], Richard[3], Serjt. John[2],
Thomas[1]), is a farmer; lived in Millbury, Mass.; removed
in the spring of 1880 to Beloit, Kansas, where he now re-
sides and has a stock farm of two hundred acres, situated on
the Solomon river.   He married, Nov. 19, 1868, Ann-Electa
Livermore, daughter of Joseph-Smith and Electa-Slocomb
Livermore, born in Sutton, Mass., April 17, 1834.

CHILD, BORN IN MILLBURY, MASS.

566.   Bessie-Florence, b. Feb. 7, 1870.

567.   WEALTHY-ISABELLA WHITE[7] [494.] (Abigail-Dennison[6] (White), William[5], Jr.. Dea. William[4], Richard[3], Serjt.
John[2], Thomas[1]), was educated at Leland Seminary, Vt.;
married, July 21, 1858, LEWIS-LAWRENCE POLLOCK, M. D.
of South Carolina; he was born in that State, Oct. 29, 1835,
and graduated at the University of Maryland in 1856.   They
now reside in Boston, Mass.

CHILDREN.

568.   Winton-Lawrence, b. May 29, 1859, in Macon, Ga.
569.   Wilhelmine-Wealthy, b. Jan. 26, 1862, in Tuscumbia, Ala.
570.   Son, b. Dec. 4, 1866, d. Aug. 30, 1867.

571.   ROLLIN-CHARLES WHITE[7] [495.] (Abigail-Dennison[6] (White), William[5], Jr.. Dea. William[4], Richard[3], Serjt.
John[2], Thomas[1]), was born in Putney, Vt.; worked on a

farm until he was twenty-one, then was engaged in chair-making for five years. In 1862 he commenced working for Thomas-H. White (no relative of his) in Templeton, Mass., in the manufacture of sewing machines. The next year the business was moved to Orange, Mass., and in Sept., 1865 to Cleveland, O. In March, 1866 Rollin-C. White[7] was made a partner in the business, and has continued in the business to the present time. The White Sewing Machine Company was formed in 1876, with Rollin-C. White[7] as vice president, which position he has since held with the exception of one year. Thomas-H. White is president. They manufacture the celebrated "White" sewing machine ; the company has a capacity for the manufacture of 2,000 machines a week, and employs about 1,000 men. He married, March 1, 1865, Lizzie-Sarah Warren, daughter of Ebenezer-C. and Olive-G. Warren, born in Hubbardston, Mass., Feb. 23, 1840.

CHILDREN, BORN IN CLEVELAND, OHIO.

572.   Fannie-Lizzie, b. Nov. 24, 1868.
573.   Fred-Rollin, b. Feb. 17, 1872.

574.   LUCRETIA-CATHERINE WHITE[7] [497.] (Abigail-Dennison[6] (White), William[5], Jr., Dea. William[4], Richard[3], Serjt. John[2], Thomas[1]), married, March 13, 1866, HENRY-FRANCIS FRANKLIN, son of James and Lucinda Franklin, born in Townshend, Vt., Oct. 30, 1840. During the Civil war he served as Corporal in Co. D, 16th Regiment Vermont Volunteers. He is a farmer, and they reside in Townshend.

CHILDREN, BORN IN TOWNSHEND, VT.

575.   Herbert-Henry, b. Feb. 16, 1868.
576.   Ernest-Rollin, b. Sept. 8, 1870.
577.   Minnie-Ruth, b. Oct. 18, 1873, d. Nov. 18, 1873.
578.   Clinton-James, b. Jan. 17, 1875.
579.   Alice-Lucretia, b. Oct. 7, 1881.

580.   FANNIE-ELLA WHITE[7] [498.] Abigail-Dennison[6] (White), William[5], Jr., Dea. William[4], Richard[3], Serjt. John[2], Thomas[1]), married, Jan. 25, 1871, FRANK-W. BARRETT, who

was born Jan. 13, 1848.   He is a farmer; they live in Beloit, Kansas.

CHILDREN, BORN IN BELOIT, KANSAS.

581.   Lizzie-May, b. Sept. 30, 1875.
582.   Alice-Inez, b. Aug. 26, 1877.
583.   Charles-Winton, b. June 29, 1880.

584.   ROLLIN-ROSWELL[7] [500.] (Christopher[6], William[5], Jr., Dea. William[4], Richard[3], Serjt. John[2], Thomas[1]), is a farmer and resides in Londonderry, Vt.   He married, May 5, 1863, Almira-L. Fisher of Londonderry, daughter of Russell-Fitch and Phebe-Almira (Skinner) Fisher, born in Grafton, Vt., Feb. 4, 1845.

CHILDREN, BORN IN LONDONDERRY, VT.

585.   Charlie-Emerson, b. May 6, 1866.
586.   Martha-Emma, b. May 15, 1875.
587.   Minnie-Etta, b. Dec. 29, 1878.

588.   ROMANZO-ALTHERON[7] [502.] (Christopher[6], William[5], Jr., Dea. William[4], Richard[3], Serjt. John[2], Thomas[1]), is a farmer and resides in Westminster, Vt.   He was in the Civil war; enlisted Jan. 13, 1862 in Co. H, 8th Regiment Vermont Volunteers; was at the siege of Port Hudson and the several battles in that vicinity, and through the campaigns under Generals Butler and Banks; remained in Louisiana until July, 1864, then the regiment was transferred to the Shenandoah valley, Va. under Gen. Sheridan.   He re-enlisted in the field Jan. 5, 1864 at New Iberia, La.; was discharged June 28, 1865 at Washington, D. C.   He married, July 7, 1867, Catharine Lanpher, daughter of John and Susan Lanpher, born in Bucksport, Me., Jan. 16, 1836.

CHILD, BORN IN LOWELL, MASS.

589.   Fred-Rome, b. May 27, 1869.

590.   AVIS-FIDELIA[7] [503.] (Christopher[6], William[5], Jr., Dea. William[4], Richard[3], Serjt. John[2], Thomas[1]), married, March 24, 1864, JOHN-WILEY JOHNSON of Townshend, Vt.,

born in Saratoga. N. Y., Sept. 4, 1838. He is a farmer, and they reside in Townshend.

CHILDREN, BORN IN TOWNSHEND, VT.

591. Emma-Fidelia, b. May 5, 1865.
592. Cora-Selucia, b. June 15, 1866, d. April 9, 1867.
593. John-Wiley, b. Sept. 6, 1871, d. Sept. 30, 1871.
594. Minnie-Avis, b. Oct. 15, 1872.
595. Grace-Jerusha, b. Jan. 13, 1875.
596. Lulu-Achsah, b. Sept. 14, 1876.

597. ACHSAH-CELESTIA[7] [505.] (Christopher[6], William[5], Jr., Dea. William[4], Richard[3], Serjt. John[2], Thomas[1]), married, May 13, 1877, DANIEL-WILLIAM DUTTON, son of Johnson-L. and Sarah-H. Dutton, born in China, Me., March 22, 1856. He is a farmer, and they reside in Townshend, Vt.

CHILDREN, BORN IN TOWNSHEND, VT.

598. William-Harris, b. July 28, 1878.
599. Guy-Ernest, b. March 3, 1880.
600. Ned-Emerson, b. April 16, 1882.

601. JULIA-ESTELLE[7] [514.] (Sylvester[6], Jasher[5], Dea. William[4], Richard[3], Serjt. John[2], Thomas[1]), married, Jan. 22, 1877, WILLIAM-JACOB BLAUVELT, who has charge of the Knickerbocker Ice Company's ice-house at Barren Island in Coeymans, N. Y., where they reside.

CHILDREN, BORN IN COEYMANS, N. Y.

602. Harry, b. May 2, 1878; lives with his great-uncle John-M. Harris[5] [see No. 524.].
603. Egbert-Stanton, b. Oct. 8, 1879.
604. Henrietta, b. Sept. 26, 1882.

605. MOSES-CLEMENT[7] [515.] (Sylvester[6], Jasher[5], Dea. William[4], Richard[3], Serjt. John[2], Thomas[1]), left his home in Coeymans, N. Y., in early life to work for his uncle George-W. Harris[6] [see No. 517.] in Lowell, Mass. "He possessed good business abilities and for some time was the chief business manager of the large manufacturing business of his uncle, and had bright and hopeful prospects of a brilliant busi-

ness career before him", but died suddenly in Lowell when about 25 years of age. He was a young man of exemplary habits, respected and loved by all who knew him.

606. JOHN-WILLIAM[7] [532.] (Solon-Hurd[6], John-Wetherby[5], Dea. William[4], Richard[3], Serjt. John[2], Thomas[1]), lives in Factory Point, Manchester, Vt., on the homestead of his father and grandfather. He owns one-half of the mill formerly owned by his father and grandfather, and there manufactures horse and army blankets, producing 2,500 pounds a week. He married, Oct. 19, 1865, Sarah Geddis, daughter of Samuel and Margaret (Densmore) Geddis, born June 6, 1847.

CHILDREN.

607. Solon, b. June 7, 1866, in Manchester, Vt., d. May 28, 1869, in Schaghticoke, N. Y.
608. Charles-Parker, b. Feb. 11, 1870, in Schaghticoke, N. Y.
609. Fannie-Etta, b. Oct. 4, 1872, in Manchester, Vt., d. Jan. 17, 1881, in Manchester, Vt.
610. Hattie-Mabel, b. Dec. 17, 1875, in Augusta, N. Y.
611. Willie-John, b. July 16, 1882, in Manchester, Vt.

612. LILLIE-LENORA RHODES[7] [538.] (Solon-Harris Rhodes[6], Ruth[5] (Rhodes), Dea. William[4], Richard[3], Serjt. John[2], Thomas[1]), married, Feb. 26, 1878, CHARLES-A. WHITNEY; they reside in Kipton, O.; he is engaged in trade there, and is constable of Camden township.

CHILDREN.

613. Myrtle-Estella, b. Aug. 12, 1879, in Pittsfield, O.
614. Claud-Harris, b. April 1, 1882, in Kipton, O.

615. JOSEPHINE-ABBIE RHODES[7] [545.] (Joseph-Warren Rhodes[6], Ruth[5] (Rhodes), Dea. William[4], Richard[3], Serjt. John[2], Thomas[1]), married, May 23, 1882, GEORGE-WASHINGTON SMELTZER, a farmer, born in Garafraxa, Wellington Co., Ontario, Canada, May 1, 1861. They live in Joyfield, Mich.

CHILD, BORN IN JOYFIELD, MICH.

616. Lida-May, b. April 1, 1883.

EIGHTH GENERATION.

617.   ELLA-HARRIS WETHERBY[8] [556.] (Catharine-Elizabeth[7] (Wetherby), Roswell[6], William[5], Jr., Dea. William[4], Richard[3], Serjt. John[2], Thomas[1]), married, Sept. 6, 1876, WILLIAM McBRIDE, a farmer: they reside in Fruit Valley, Oswego Co., N. Y.

CHILD, BORN IN OSWEGO, N. Y.

618.   Howard, b. Aug. 4, 1878. He is in the *ninth generation* in America from Thomas Harris[1]. (See Nos. 227½, 620.)

619.   JAMES-ROSWELL WETHERBY[8] [557.] (Catharine-Elizabeth[7] (Wetherby), Roswell[6], William[5], Jr., Dea. William[4], Richard[3], Serjt. John[2], Thomas[1]), is a carpenter and school-teacher, and resides with his parents in Victory, N. Y. He married, Nov. 25, 1880, Mariette Evans, who died in Victory, March 17, 1882.

CHILD, BORN IN VICTORY, N. Y.

620.   Evans-James, b. March 11, 1882. He is in the *ninth generation* in America from Thomas Harris[1]. (See Nos. 227½, 618.)

ADDITIONS.

Page 19. (No. 4.) Samuel⁵. He was probably the one who died in Byfield parish, Newbury, Mass., Jan. 29, 1770, "almost 75; he had no family there, but lived with his son-in-law John Webber". (Byfield Church Records.) John Webber married Rachel Harris, March 15, 1759, in Rowley, Mass.

Page 38. No. 51. Dea. Jacob⁶, Jr. The following is the closing portion of a poem of ten stanzas written by him, dated "Windham, July 23, 1833":—

> "A few more fleeting years roll on,
> And life's important work is done,
> What though it be a thorny road,
> That leads us onward to our God.
>
> "Lo! in the heavens a building stands,
> Reared up by uncreated hands;
> 'Twas purchased by the Eternal Son,
> And chartered to the saints alone.
>
> "Oh! may we join the throng above,
> And sing redeeming grace and love,
> When earth with all its toils and cares
> No more attracts, no more ensnares.
>
> "Adieu! adieu! to things below,
> When Jesus calls we all must go,
> And when the trump shall raise the dead,
> May we arise in Christ our head."

Page 53. No. 135½. Son. He is named Frank-William.

Page 54. No. 140. Edward-Melville. The facts can not be ascertained, but Serjt. John[2] and Thomas[1] *may* have been members of the church in Ipswich, (if so, making *eight* generations,) as the will of each contains indications of a personal faith in Christ.

Page 63. No. 175. Clarinda Whitney[6] (Woodbury). She is the oldest of the descendants of Richard Harris[3] now living. Two others, born before 1800, are now (Aug., 1883) living.—Nos. 53 and 59.

INDEX I.

— — —

TO NAMES OF HARRISES IN PART I. (CHAPTERS I, II, III).

NAME.	PAGE.
Agnes[4], dau. of John[3],	21
Ann[1], m. Elias Maverick,	8
Anthony[1],	8
Arthur, 1640,	7
Daniel[1],	8
Daniel[3], son of Serjt. John[2],	19
Ebenezer[2], son of Thomas[1],	14
Elizabeth[2], dau. of Thomas[1], m. John Gallup,	13
George, 1636,	7
Giles[4], son of John[3]	21
John[1],	8
John[2], Serjt., son of Thomas[1],	13, 18
John[3], son of Serjt. John[2],	19, 20
John[4], son of John[3],	20
Margaret[2], dau. of Thomas[1], m. John Staniford,	14
Martha[2], dau of Thomas[1],	13
Martha[3], dau. of Serjt. John[2],	19, 21
Mary[2], dau. of Thomas[1],	14
Rebecca[3], dau. of Serjt. John[2], m. William Wilcomb,	19, 21
Richard[3], son of Serjt. John[2],	19, 21
Samuel[3], son of Serjt. John[2],	19, 127
Thomas and Elizabeth, 1630,	7
Thomas, 1637,	7
Thomas[1], m. Martha Lake,	8, 9
Thomas[2], son of Thomas[1],	13
Walter, 1632,	7
William, 1635,	7
William[1],	8
William[2], son of Thomas[1],	14
William[3], son of Serjt. John[2],	19

INDEX II.

TO NAMES OF DESCENDANTS OF RICHARD HARRIS[2], (IN PART II).

NAME.	ANCESTOR.	NO.	PAGE.
Allen, William-H.[7],	*Richard*[4]. *Jr.*	222	71
Beckwith, Eloise-L.[7],	*Rebecca*[4] (*Scollay*).	265	78
Beckwith, James-F.[7],	*Rebecca*[4] (*Scollay*).	310	83
Beckwith, Lawrence-B.[7],	*Rebecca*[4] (*Scollay*).	264	78
Beckwith, Mary-E.[7],	*Rebecca*[4] (*Scollay*).	265[1/2]	78
Beckwith, Sally-M.[7], m. Baylor.	*Rebecca*[4] (*Scollay*).	311	84
Beckwith, Samuel-S.[7],	*Rebecca*[4] (*Scollay*).	261	78
Bowen, Anna-C.-M.[7],	*Nathaniel*[4].	388	95
Bowen, Caroline-F.[7], m. Fairbanks.	*Nathaniel*[4],	426	102
Bowen, Ella-H.[7], m. McFarland.	*Nathaniel*[4],	441	103
Bowen, Fannie-M.[7], m. Waldo.	*Nathaniel*[4],	422	102
Bowen, Louise[7], m. Ballard.	*Nathaniel*[4],	432	102
Brick, Francis[7], Dr.,	*Rebecca*[4] (*Scollay*).	329	87
Brick, Harriet-S.[7], m. Wilson.	*Rebecca*[4] (*Scollay*).	331	87
Draper, Albert-J.-R.[7],	*Nathaniel*[4],	413	101
Draper, George-H.[7],	*Nathaniel*[4],	411	101
Farnsworth, Dorothy[6], m. Chase.	*Rebecca*[4]. (*Scollay*)	306	82
Farnsworth, Ezra-S.[6],	*Rebecca*[4] (*Scollay*).	308	82
Farrand, Caroline-A.[7], m. Morgan.	*Nathaniel*[4].	410	100
Farrand, Ellen-S.[7], m. Chase.	*Nathaniel*[4].	408	99
Farrand, Martha-C.[7], m. Doolittle.	*Nathaniel*[4].	404	99
Harris, Abigail-D.[6]. m. White and Gates,	*William*[4].	491	108
Harris, Achsah-C.[7], m. Dutton,	*William*[4].	597	124
Harris, Amanda-B.[6],	*Richard*[4]. *Jr.*	188	66
Harris, Asenath[5], m. Whitney.	*Richard*[4]. *Jr.*.	154	60
Harris, Augustus-G.[6],	*Richard*[4]. *Jr.*.	189	68
Harris, Avis-F.[7], m. Johnson.	*William*[4]	590	123
Harris, Betsey-M.[6], m. Mott,	*Nathaniel*[4].	378	94
Harris, Betsy[5], m. Merriam.	*Jacob*[3].	25	34
Harris, Caroline-M.[6],	*William*[4].	470	106
Harris, Catharine-E.[7], m. Wetherby.	*William*[4].	555	120

NAME.	ANCESTOR.	NO.	PAGE.
Harris, Catherine[6], m. Little.	Richard[4], Jr.,	172	63
Harris, Cemantha-O.[7],	William[4].	510	110
Harris, Charles[6]. (son of John-W.[5].)	William[4].	533	115
Harris, Charles[6]. (son of William[5], Jr.,)	William[4].	512	110
Harris, Charles-C.[7].	Jacob[4].	73	42
Harris, Charles-E.[6].	Nathaniel[4]	366	93
Harris, Charlotte-E.[7].	Jacob[4]	75	43
Harris, Charlotte-H.[6], m. Allen.	Richard[4], Jr.,	185	64
Harris, Christopher[6].	William[4].	499	109
Harris, Cornelia-W.[6].	William[4].	478	107
Harris, Cynthia-L.[6], m. Parker.	Nathaniel[4].	356	91
Harris, Edward-M.[5],	Jacob[4],	140 (128)	54
Harris, Edward-P.[6],	Jacob[4].	60	40
Harris, Edward-W.[7], Judge.	Jacob[4].	106	47
Harris, Edwin-A.[7],	Jacob[4].	125	51
Harris, Elizabeth[6], m. Underhill.	Jacob[4].	77	43
Harris, Eliza-H.[7], m. Peakes,	Jacob[4],	120	50
Harris, Eliza-P.[6].	Richard[4], Jr.,	152	60
Harris, Eunice[5].	Jacob[4],	52	38
Harris, Francis-T.[6].	William[4].	530	115
Harris, Franklin[6].	Richard[4], Jr.,	193	68
Harris, Fred-A.[7].	William[4].	511	110
Harris, George[6].	Richard[4], Jr.,	171	63
Harris, George-W.[6],	William[4].	517	111
Harris, George-W.[7].	Jacob[4].	122	51
Harris, Hannah-A.[6], m. Draper.	Nathaniel[4].	372	94
Harris, Harrison-G.[5],	Richard[4], Jr.,	163	61
Harris, Haswell[5].	Nathaniel[4].	364	93
Harris, Henry-L.[6].	Richard[4], Jr.,	196	69
Harris, Hubbard-C.[6].	William[4].	525	114
Harris, Jacob[4], Dea..	Richard[3].	17	31
Harris, Jacob[5], Jr., Dea..	Jacob[4].	51 (127)	38
Harris, Jacob[6].	Jacob[4].	74	43
Harris, Jasher[5].	William[4].	459	106
Harris, Joel[5].	Richard[4], Jr.,	157	60
Harris, John[5], Judge.	Richard[4], Jr.,	149	57
Harris, John-A.[6].	Richard[4], Jr.,	187	64
Harris, John-M.[5], Dea..	Jacob[4].	71	41
Harris, John-M.[6].	William[4].	524	113
Harris, John-W.[5],	William[4].	471	106
Harris, John-W.[7].	William[4].	606	125
Harris, John-W.[7].	Jacob[4].	69	41
Harris, Jonas[6].	William[4].	508	110

NAME.	ANCESTOR.	NO.	PAGE.
Harris, Joseph-L.[7],	*Nathaniel*[4],	402	98
Harris, Julia-E.[7], m. Blauvelt.	*William*[4],	601	124
Harris, Julius-O.[6],	*Nathaniel*[4],	360	91
Harris, Lillie-E.[8],	*Jacob*[4],	139	54
Harris, Luther[5],	*Jacob*[4],	79	44
Harris, Lydia-G.[6], m. Case,	*Nathaniel*[4],	389	95
Harris, Lydia-K.[6], m. Dearborn,	*Jacob*[4],	76	43
Harris, Marilla-A.[6], m. Wilbur.	*William*[4],	516	111
Harris, Martha[4], m. Wetherbee,	*Richard*[3],	12	29
Harris, Martha[5], m. Moore.	*Jacob*[4],	46	37
Harris, Martha[5],	*William*[4],	446	105
Harris, Mary-A.[6],	*William*[4],	469	106
Harris, Mary-B.[6],	*Richard*[4], *Jr.*,	195	68
Harris, Mary-C.[7],	*Nathaniel*[4],	403	99
Harris, Mary-N.[6], m. Farrand.	*Nathaniel*[4],	368	93
Harris, Mary-W.[6],	*Jacob*[4],	35	37
Harris, Moses-C.[7],	*William*[4],	605	124
Harris, Nathaniel[4],	*Richard*[3],	333	88
Harris, Nathaniel[5], Jr.,	*Nathaniel*[4],	343	89
Harris, Otis[7],	*Nathaniel*[4],	395	98
Harris, Rebecca[4], m. Scollay.	*Richard*[3],	229	73
Harris, Richard[3],		1	25
Harris, Richard[4], Jr., Dea..	*Richard*[3],	141	56
Harris, Richard[5],	*Nathaniel*[4],	350	90
Harris, Rollin-R.[7],	*William*[4],	584	123
Harris, Romanzo-A.[7],	*William*[4],	588	123
Harris, Rosaline[7], m. Swasey.	*Nathaniel*[4],	393	97
Harris, Roswell[6],	*William*[4],	489	108
Harris, Rufus[5],	*Nathaniel*[4],	345	90
Harris, Ruth[5], m. Rhodes.	*William*[4],	479	107
Harris, Sally[5],	*Jacob*[4],	21	32
Harris, Sally[5] or Sarah[5],	*Richard*[4], *Jr.*.	147	57
Harris, Sally[6], m. Coult.	*Jacob*[4],	59	39
Harris, Samuel[5], Rev .	*Jacob*[4],	33	34
Harris, Samuel[6],	*Jacob*[4],	63	40
Harris, Samuel[7],	*Jacob*[4],	115	49
Harris, Sarah-H.[6],	*William*[4],	473	106
Harris, Sarah-L.[6], m. Bowen.	*Nathaniel*[4],	384	95
Harris, Solon-H.[6],	*William*[4],	531	115
Harris, Sylvester[6],	*William*[4],	513	110
Harris, William[4], Dea..	*Richard*[3],	444	104
Harris, William[5], Jr..	*William*[4],	450	105
Harris, William-C.[6], Dea..	*Jacob*[4],	80	44
Harris, William-R.[6],	*William*[4],	523	113

NAME.	ANCESTOR.	NO.	PAGE.
Harris, William-S.[7],	*Jacob*[4].	136	53
Mann, Albert-E.[7],	*Richard*[4], *Jr.*,	227	72
Mann, Clara-E.[7], m. Burgess.	*Richard*[4], *Jr.*,	228	72
Mann, Julia-L.[7], m. Kempton.	*Richard*[4], *Jr.*	226	72
Mann, Oliver-L.[7],	*Richard*[4], *Jr.*,	205	70
Merriam, Betsey[6], m. Harris.	*Jacob*[4].	58	39
Merriam, Ellen-A.[7], m. Prescott.	*Jacob*[4].	96	46
Merriam, Jacob-H.[6],	*Jacob*[4].	53	39
Merriam, Lyman-W.[7],	*Jacob*[4].	98	47
Merriam, Mary-E.[7],	*Jacob*[4].	54	39
Merriam, Sally-H.[6],	*Jacob*[4].	29	34
Moore, Cordelia-E.[6], m. Sprague.	*Jacob*[4].	88	45
Moore, Emily[6].	*Jacob*[4].	47	38
Moore, John-M.[6].	*Jacob*[4].	94	45
Moore, Marius-H[6].	*Jacob*[4],	84	45
Moore, Samuel-S.[7].	*Rebecca*[4] (*Scollay*),	343	84
Moore, Wilbur-F.[7].	*Jacob*[4],	86	45
Moore, William-E.[7].	*Jacob*[4],	85	45
Mott, Charles-A.[7],	*Nathaniel*[4].	418	101
Mott, Julius-H.[7].	*Nathaniel*[4].	414	104
Nellis, Walter-P.[7].	*Nathaniel*[4].	392	97
Page, Sally-S.[7].	*Rebecca*[4] (*Scollay*).	271	79
Parker, Edwin-R.[7].	*Nathaniel*[4].	390	96
Parker, Eliza[7], m. Smith.	*Rebecca*[4] (*Scollay*).	317	85
Parker, Sarah[7], m. Nellis.	*Nathaniel*[4].	391	96
Parks, Flora-J.[7].	*Richard*[4], *Jr.*,	211	71
Pollock, Wilhelmine-W.[7].	*William*[4].	569	121
Pollock, Winton-L.[7].	*William*[4].	568	121
Rhodes, Abigail-E.[6], m. McClelland.	*William*[4].	535	116
Rhodes, Alice-E.[7].	*William*[4].	543	118
Rhodes, Charles-H.[7].	*William*[4].	540	118
Rhodes, Francis-N.[7],	*William*[4],	539	118
Rhodes, Harriet-M.[6], m. Loree.	*William*[4].	534	116
Rhodes, Hattie-L.[7].	*William*[4].	546	119
Rhodes, Isaac-N.[6].	*William*[4].	552	119
Rhodes, Josephine-A.[7], m. Smeltzer.	*William*[4].	615	125
Rhodes, Joseph-W.[6].	*William*[4].	542	118
Rhodes, Lillie-L.[7], m. Whitney.	*William*[4].	612	125
Rhodes, Solon-H.[6].	*William*[4].	537	117
Rhodes, William-H.[6].	*William*[4].	549	119
Sargent, Edwin-H.[7].	*Richard*[4], *Jr.*,	216	71
Sargent, George-A.[7].	*Richard*[4], *Jr.*,	217	71
Scollay, Abel[4].	*Rebecca*[4] (*Scollay*).	255	77
Scollay, Anne-L.[6], m. Beckwith.	*Rebecca*[4] (*Scollay*).	259	78

NAME.	ANCESTOR.	NO.	PAGE.
Scollay, Charles⁶,	*Rebecca⁴ (Scollay),*	304	81
Scollay, Charles⁷,	*Rebecca⁴ (Scollay),*	327	86
Scollay, Charles-L.⁶, Dr.,	*Rebecca⁴ (Scollay),*	258	78
Scollay, Dolly⁶, m. Whitney.	*Rebecca⁴ (Scollay),*	291	81
Scollay, Eleanor-G.⁶, m. Moore.	*Rebecca⁴ (Scollay),*	266	78
Scollay, Elizabeth⁶, m. Page.	*Rebecca⁴ (Scollay),*	270	79
Scollay, Emma-B.⁷, m. Beehler.	*Rebecca⁴ (Scollay),*	320	85
Scollay, Ezra⁵,	*Rebecca⁴ (Scollay),*	251	77
Scollay, Harriot-L.⁶, m. Evans.	*Rebecca⁴ (Scollay),*	273	79
Scollay, James⁵,	*Rebecca⁴ (Scollay),*	244	76
Scollay, James⁶, Jr.,	*Rebecca⁴ (Scollay),*	296	81
Scollay, James⁷, Jr.,	*Rebecca⁴ (Scollay),*	325	86
Scollay, Lucy⁵, m. Farnsworth.	*Rebecca⁴ (Scollay),*	252	77
Scollay, Lucy⁶, m. Brick.	*Rebecca⁴ (Scollay),*	302	82
Scollay, Lucy-M.⁷, m. Glazier.	*Rebecca⁴ (Scollay),*	319	85
Scollay, Mary-N.⁶, m. Nelson.	*Rebecca⁴ (Scollay),*	281	80
Scollay, Samuel⁵, Dr.,	*Rebecca⁴ (Scollay),*	235	75
Scollay, Sarah⁶, m. Parker.	*Rebecca⁴ (Scollay),*	294	81
Sprague, Anna-M.⁷,	*Jacob⁴,*	90	45
Sprague, Edward-F.⁷,	*Jacob⁴,*	92	45
Sprague, Hattie-E.⁷,	*Jacob⁴,*	91	45
Sprague, Mary-C.⁷, m. Fuller.	*Jacob⁴,*	137	54
Underhill, George-C.⁷,	*Jacob⁴,*	133	52
Wetherbee, Eunice⁵,	*Martha⁴ (Wetherbee),*	16	29
Wetherbee, Jacob⁵,	*Martha⁴ (Wetherbee),*	15	29
Wetherbee, Martha⁵,	*Martha⁴ (Wetherbee),*	13	29
Wetherbee, Richard⁵,	*Martha⁴ (Wetherbee),*	14	29
Wetherby, Clarence-A.⁷,	*William⁴,*	558	120
Wetherby, Ella-H.⁷, m. McBride.	*William⁴,*	617	126
Wetherby, James-R.⁷,	*William⁴,*	619	126
White, Abby-A.⁷, m. Winslow.	*William⁴,*	562	121
White, Fannie-E.⁷, m. Barrett.	*William⁴,*	580	122
White, Lucretia-C.⁷, m. Franklin.	*William⁴,*	574	122
White, Newel-H.⁷,	*William⁴,*	565	121
White, Rollin-C.⁷,	*William⁴,*	571	121
White, Ruth-A.⁷,	*William⁴,*	496	108
White, Wealthy-I.⁷, m. Pollock.	*William⁴,*	567	121
Whitney, Charles⁷,	*Rebecca⁴ (Scollay),*	315	85
Whitney, Clarinda⁶, m. Woodbury,	*Richard⁴, Jr.,*	175 (128)	63
Winslow, George-P.⁷,	*William⁴,*	563	121
Woodbury, Andrew-C.⁷,	*Richard⁴, Jr.,*	184	64
Woodbury, Asenath-H.⁷, m. Mann.	*Richard⁴, Jr.,*	198	70
Woodbury, Clarinda-A.⁷, m. Sargent.	*Richard⁴, Jr.,*	215	71
Woodbury, Lauretta-W.⁷, m. Parks.	*Richard⁴, Jr.,*	210	70

NAME.	ANCESTOR.	NO.	PAGE.
Woodbury, Lucinda-B.[7], m. Newman,	*Richard*[6], *Jr.*,	212	71
Woodbury, Maria-A.[7], m. Wallace,	*Richard*[6], *Jr.*,	219	71
Woodbury, Mary-A.[7], m. Page,	*Richard*[6], *Jr.*,	206	70
Woodbury, Nathan-G.[7],	*Richard*[6], *Jr.*,	208	70